About the Author

William Dumont is an author who resides in Wantagh, NY, with his wife, Bee. He is very happily married and has raised three children. He recently retired after thirty-four years in education. He has served as a teacher, assistant principal of science, coach and athletic director. He hopes to have a long and wonderful retirement and continue to use the newfound time in retirement in many creative endeavors!

The Canarsee, Stones and Justice

William Dumont

The Canarsee, Stones and Justice

Olympia Publishers
London

www.olympiapublishers.com
OLYMPIA PAPERBACK EDITION

Copyright © William Dumont 2024

The right of William Dumont to be identified as author of
this work has been asserted in accordance with sections 77 and 78 of
the Copyright, Designs and Patents Act 1988.

All Rights Reserved

No reproduction, copy or transmission of this publication
may be made without written permission.
No paragraph of this publication may be reproduced,
copied or transmitted save with the written permission of the publisher,
or in accordance with the provisions
of the Copyright Act 1956 (as amended).

Any person who commits any unauthorized act in relation to
this publication may be liable to criminal
prosecution and civil claims for damage.

A CIP catalogue record for this title is
available from the British Library.

ISBN: 978-1-80439-344-4

This is a work of fiction.
Names, characters, places and incidents originate from the writer's
imagination. Any resemblance to actual persons, living or dead, is
purely coincidental.

First Published in 2024

**Olympia Publishers
Tallis House
2 Tallis Street
London
EC4Y 0AB**

Printed in Great Britain

Dedication

The book is dedicated to all who dreamed of crazy adventures wrapped in a riddle.

Acknowledgments

I was always a bit nervous about writing this story. I would never have undertaken this project without the constant support of my wife, Barbara! Thank you for being my lovable guiding bear!

So many people visit special, historical or sacred places. Some just walk around and take in the view. Others stare off and take an introspective view. Some are completely unimpressed and bored. A few, a very few, go to these places hoping for an out of body experience. Maybe they make an attempt to try to feel the past. Some claim they do make a connection. Others mock it.

For a high school kid named Ray Alford, the past was going to be a life changing event he never thought possible…

In the very early 1600s, a band of the Canarsee lived very happily in what would become the land of Brooklyn, NY. They thrived on the shores of Jamaica Bay. Men hunted and fished while the woman raised their families. The Canarsee were at peace with their place in the world. One of the advantages of living by Jamaica Bay was the challenges it offered. Young boys had to take the challenge of canoeing up the bay to lower Manhattan and hunt. For those who do not know the area, this is a long and hard canoe ride to do. The currents are very strong in this area of what we call today NYC. If the young person reached lower Manhattan and the hunt was successful, they were accepted as men in the brotherhood of the tribe. Little did they know that the stirrings in an alien world was about to change all of their lives for the worst.

The chief of the tribe, Chief Gouwane, was a good man. He was a man with a love for humanity. His wife, Chieftess Tantaqua was pregnant. They both were hoping for a son. Sometimes, the Chief would insist that she attend a meeting with the medicine man, Danckaerts. The Chief had a strong belief in his medicine man. He had a true faith in him. The Chieftess however did not. While woman generally did not attend any of the medicine man's meetings or spiritual rituals, the Chief would sometimes insist his Chieftess attend. Danckaerts was a man who many believed had a connection to the spiritual world. Some were non-believers and others like Chief Gouwane truly believed he had a connection. The Chieftess, after some prompting by the Chief, decided to attend a dancing ritual where the spirits of the Menitto appeared and confirmed special powers, protection or a foreboding about what is to come. The Menitto were ghosts of the past Canarsee people who still roamed the earth always trying to help their families. Tantaqua was always doubtful and did not have the faith that her husband and others had. Still, she decided to go to the ritual and give it a try. What did she have to lose?

Turns out she had much to lose…

As Danckaerts was preparing for the ritual, both the Chief and Chieftess arrived. It was obvious to Danckaerts that the Chief was full of faith while Chieftess Tantaqua was not. Danckaerts told the Chieftess that this would be a night both her and her unborn child will always remember. She was visibly agitated after this statement; however she kept some composure and took her proper place as the ritual began. A great fire was burning as they sat in a circle with other tribal members. Danckaerts danced all around the fire. The music had a rhythm that was quite uplifting and hopeful. The music suddenly turned dark and Danckaerts blew a powder into the flames and all saw nothing except for the Chieftess. She jumped to her feet as the others stared at her with a surprised look. The Chief was somewhat elated in the moment that his wife was having a spiritual moment. While publicly he would never discuss it, privately he wished that Tantaqua was more open to the spirits.

When the Chieftess appeared to stop seeing her vision, all stopped. No dancing, no music. A time of complete silence was given for the Chieftess to interpret her vision. The vision revealed what she believed to be numbers; nine, six, zero and one. Then her "Menitto" appeared to her above the flames. It presented itself as a family member from the deep past. While she did not have any knowledge of the person, she was surprised at how much she looked like herself. The "Menitto" showed her a future with a strange looking alien ship surrounded by pain with a darkness that had an end. The end of the darkness revealed the end of her child and family. The more she processed the vision, the more angry she became. She decided she needed to be alone. She fled from all and ran deep into the forest. The Chief prevented all from following her and wanted her to process whatever experience she had.

Tantaqua ran for miles. She was six months pregnant. She was filled with rage, worry, fear and a sense of hopelessness. She stopped at small grassland with a view of Jamaica Bay. Today, this would be a bit west of Marine Park in Brooklyn, NY. She sat down and looked at the full moon. She was taught to use the moon as a way of keeping time but nothing she thought of made any sense at this time. All she held as real was brought into question after actually seeing her vision.

What did these numbers mean? What was the alien? Who was the alien? Where did this weird ship come from? All she could do was look at her belly and rub it. She cried in fear for her unborn child. She also tried to talk herself into believing nothing really happened. While it did not work, it was comforting to her a bit. She built a fire and planned to scratch out on a rock what she saw to help her think. As she was looking for a stone for the job, she found a somewhat pretty stone with a red, blue and green streak on the top. It also had a gray center and it appeared to be a tough stone. She picked it up and scratched with all her energy into a large stone the numbers nine, six, zero and one. She scratched what she believed to be a picture of the alien ship. She closed her eyes and ran the numbers and the alien ship in her mind with the darkness. Nothing came to mind. She slept and returned to her settlement in the morning leaving the pretty rock and her numbers on the larger rock.

The Chief, her husband, could not wait to hear about her vision. As she told him, every word seemed to mean more to him than her. The Chief started to cry. She could not understand why? The vision has no meaning to me. How can this story make you cry? The Chief revealed that he has had the exact same vision many times from his "Menitto." He went to their home and showed her his drawings on deer skin. They were almost identical to the drawings she scratched out on the rock. They stared at each other. The Chief believed this was the end for his people and his unborn son would be the end of the tribe. Tantaqua would have none of it and believed it was all a trick being played for a reason she could never give...

As summer turned to fall, Tantaqua was to give birth to a beautiful young healthy boy. The year was 1609, using the European time keeping format. As they cleaned and wrapped the newborn child, a large stirring was taking place in the village. The Chief ran out to the bay and was told by people who were fishing in Jamaica Bay that they saw something they never saw before. They all tried to explain to the Chief but the Chief could not believe what he was being told. He demanded to get their fastest canoe and take him to this sight. As they paddled toward the end of Jamaica Bay, the Chief saw an alien ship. A giant ship filled with people very different from him. Some were yelling to him in a language he never heard. They remained a safe distance away from the ship. The Chief just stared at the ship as it sailed up the river on the side of what today is Manhattan. Today the river is called the Hudson River. They all returned to share what they had seen and what it could mean. The Chief knew this was exactly what he has seen in his vision. He was filled with sadness but did not share his knowledge with anyone.

Tantaqua was lying down as she went into labor. She gave birth to her son very quickly. She wanted to hold her newborn son and she demanded to. As she laid on the ground with her newborn son, she stared into his eyes and refused to allow or believe that anything but a great future was in store for the future Chief and her people. She loved his shiny brown eyes and decided to name him after a young deer – Mamalis.

As the men returned from the bay, a large stirring was taking place in the village. All discussed what they saw. Fear, surprise, wonder and worry were all expressed. Tantaqua could not believe what she was hearing. After all, she did not see it with her own eyes. She was just taking it all in and trying to make sense out what must have been wild tales to her about different looking people with a massive floating ship. As the days past, the "alien ship" was far gone. It sailed up the Hudson River. Words from various tribes reached the Canarsee about this ship. The future chief was growing and quite healthy. His mom was getting her strength back every day. As all continued to talk about this, an elder member of the tribe discussed a similar story that he heard from his older family members about a very similar ship that came around seventy-five years ago. Nothing was made of it. Just talk and that ship came and went just like this ship did. A few years past and the story and thoughts about this "alien ship" became a great topic of discussion and wonder but never any answers.

In keeping with the European time format, the year 1611 arrived and a few ships arrived at Lower Manhattan. The Canarsee were doing what they always did. Canoeing and fishing in the bay. They saw and recognized the same shape of the ship they saw before. They watched what appeared to be alien looking people starting a small settlement on the southern tip of their land in modern day Manhattan. A tribal meeting was demanded by many and the Chief agreed to have a meeting that night. All the obvious opinions were expressed. Attack, fear, invasion while others felt that they needed to be watched so that a war plan could be created. Some advocated for an alliance with other tribes to push out the invaders of their lands.

Chief Gouwane did not speak as all expressed their opinions and feelings. He also allowed Chieftess Tantaqua to stand beside him during this meeting. This appeared to infuriate many; however, he did not allow her to move. She remained next to him as silent as him while listening intently to all. After a very long time, the Chief stood up and stated that they needed more information about this ship and the strange looking people who have arrived. He ordered his warriors to observe in secret all they could for a month and to report back to him with all they had discovered. The Chief and the Chieftess still did not dare share their vision with anyone. They were hoping it was just not true.

The new settlers had no idea how much they were being observed. They did see what appeared to them as strange looking people in their canoes. The Canarsee had looking posts all over Brooklyn. They were constantly watching what was going on. For those who do not know, what is downtown Brooklyn today has a clear view to lower Manhattan. Much can be seen from this vantage point. The reports all seemed to be the same. The "aliens" had many items that appeared to be used as tools and a different weapon that "shot smoke." They were obsessed with getting as many animal pelts as they could. However, the Canarsee observed that they were not very good hunters and did not know how to obtain all that they wanted. As this was explained to the Chief, he made a decision that set a course that would eventually be questioned by many. He decided to make contact and trade for these new items for the pelts that we are able to get with relative ease. Was his decision right? Would war have been better? If they destroyed the new settlement would more come? He remembered the old men telling all that his family saw a ship like this seventy-five years ago. The Chief believed that this was something that would not go away for now. He tried to create a place where his tribe could continue to thrive and the new people could live.

The members of the Canarsee tribe had tremendous respect for Chief Gouwane. He had proven himself to be a caring and great leader. They followed his wishes and took their canoes to make first contact. Take a moment and try to imagine this scene. A bunch of Canarsee canoeing to lower Manhattan, getting out of the canoe and walking into a European camp. Fear, worry, surprise and even communication must have been real issues. Somehow, communication began and both sides traded their goods at whatever deals were made that day. Tantaqua could not shake the vision she had, nor the numbers on the rock. The last few years has seemed like a new reality filled with more questions, worry and wonder than answers. Her son has been growing into a strong little boy. She would stare at him and wonder and worry about his future. She loved the life she had lived and was worried that this new people would change everything. She had a strong sense that disaster was coming. However, no sign of it existed so she would just try to stop thinking about it and live each day.

In the European year of 1624, The Chief acquired a disease that no one saw before. He had many flu-like symptoms. He decided to leave the village and go for a walk and be alone as he rested and recovered. He walked on the same path Tantaqua took many years ago. He even found the stone that Tantaqua scratched the numbers nine, six, zero and one on. He saw and held the uniquely colored stone she used to carve the numbers on the large rock. He built a camp by the stone and decided to stay there until he felt better. He was happy to see that his wife did take her vision from the "Menitto" more seriously than he ever knew. He sat there for days trying as she did to make sense out of the numbers. Each day, more and more infections appeared on his skin. Unknown to the Chief, he now had smallpox. Since he decided to be alone during his convalescence, no one else got the disease. He passed alone at the stone. Right before he passed he grasp the strange colored stone and thought about his wife and son. He was worried. The strange disease that was overtaking him made him believe it came from the new people. He worried but was too weak to walk back and tell his people. As he passed the red color of the stone lit up a bit and shined for a brief moment. The Chief saw this, smiled as if he understood the meaning of it and passed alone.

It was some time before the Chief's body was discovered. Many had an idea that he had passed, but once the discovery was made the tribe mourned. His body was taken back for a proper burial. The stone dropped from his hand as they took his body back. No one paid any attention to the stone or the numbers scratched on the rock. It was a time for mourning. Tantaqua was filled with shock and worry. Her son would now be the new Chief. He was only fifteen years old. As he was installed into the new position, she was worried that he was too young to comprehend all that was going on and make wise decisions. She was comforted by the fact that her relationship with her son was excellent and he did worship his father. As the tribe recovered from the Chief's strange death, the following year the strange people built a very large fort on the island of Manhattan. Tantaqua decided to paddle in her canoe to see it. It appeared to be a massive structure to her. As she paddled around southern Manhattan, she noticed the different looking people waving to her. She wanted to land but she was too worried about what may happen to her. She knew that her young son, the new Chief, would need her guidance for some time. As she paddled and just observed all, one of the ships had the numbers, 1609, on the side of it. A streak of fear overwhelmed her. She paddled toward the ship that was docked with these strange numbers. She stopped and just stared at them. She remembered the numbers shown to her from her "Menitto" nine, six, zero, and one. She gasp as she rearranged them in her mind to 1609. Men on the ship saw her and threw a blanket to her. She caught it and paddled away. When she arrived back at her camp, she immediately hiked to the rock where she scratched the numbers. She happened to sit where her husband passed. She found the pretty colored yet strange rock again on the floor. She picked it up again and stared at the numbers. She was angry at not making the connection before this day. But how could she? European years were not the way she counted years. She didn't even know that it was a year. She just knew the numbers appeared in her "Menitto" and her husband died with some strange looking bumps on him. She was overwhelmed with emotion and decided to camp there. The Chief's old campsite was untouched. The tent was still there. Each day she got more and more flu like symptoms. The same white marks started to appear on her body like her husband. She understood that this disease came from the new people. She was too weak to walk back and tell her people and, most of all, her son, the Chief. She sat there holding the uniquely colored rock and passed away. As she passed holding the stone, the green part of the stone lit up brightly. She was not worried. It appeared as if she understood all now. As she passed alone in the same manner as her husband did, she appeared to be at peace as the stone dropped from her hand. She was discovered many days later. The tribe mourned her passing and knew that their new Chief needed her more than ever. Chief Mamalis was now all alone to face a future full of trouble.

As the time past, many of the surrounding Native Americans were dying from this new disease. Many wanted to fight against the new people. Many skirmishes did occur. Many Native Americans died. However, the disease was the major killer. The young Chief did realize the numbers in his tribe were dropping each month from this disease. He called a council for advice. Like his father before, he sat silent and listened to all. It was agreed to be part of a larger group and sell the land to the new people. He went with a large group to make this offer. The deal was made and the Chief came back with many supplies.

He took the same walk that his parents did and discovered the rock with the numbers. He was never told about the visions his parents had. He sat there and stared at the numbers as his parents did before him. He held the strange colored stone and flipped it up and down in his hand. He missed his parents deeply and wondered why he was chosen for this path in life. He slept in the same tent his parents did at the large stone. Stared at the numbers, nine, six, zero and one. He stared at the picture of the ship. Each day he felt worse. He stayed at the campsite. The same strange white infections appeared over his body as he tossed the stone in his hand for comfort. As he passed holding the stone, the blue part of the stone glowed. He was very fearful as he noticed this. Then a wave of peace overtook him. All the colors of the stone glowed – blue, green and red. The middle also glowed with a brownish yellow that seem to match his eye color. Chief Mamalis passed away alone and the stone dropped to the ground. Eventually, the Canarsee were no more. Disease, war and the inevitable arrival of more and more Europeans made their way of life and their existence a thing of the past.

29

Time is a very strange thing when you actually sit down to ponder how it works on humans. We always hear people state they "always remember." Sometimes it's a loved one. Maybe a tragedy or special event. In all cases it is almost always applied to our everyday lives. The world at this time has six to seven billion people. Do we remember any of them from the year seven hundred A.D.? Eight hundred A.D.? Tragedies that occurred in the twelfth century? We may remember or believe we remember in our lifetime all that we hold dear. However, as each generation passes, what they hold dear inevitably will be something that the new generation does not. As the years pass, so does the tragedy. Maybe this is a good thing for humanity? Maybe not? This is for you to decide.

As time marches on, the land grows and changes. It hides the past and weather washes away many remnants of the past. The strange rocks that were buried near the large stone over time disappeared for the moment. While they did glow from time to time, no one knew since they were buried. The large stone stood firmly against the weather. Rain, snow and the occasional lightning hit the stone. Who knew what it would do to the strange colored stone buried right next to it? All seemed lost to time. No one would know the tragedy that occurred and the strange rocks that touched three people.

Time also seems to wash away what the past looked like. As we live our lives, we seem to believe it was always this way.

Streets, cities, homes all feel like they were here "forever." If you ask people in Brooklyn, NY today about the Canarsee Native Americans they will all be shocked to learn that NYC was once home to many Native American tribes. Brooklyn, the most populous borough of NYC, was quite rural less than a hundred years ago. The city decided to build very large high schools in Canarsie during the late 1920s and 30s. The land was open and people were just starting to push east. All happened without any thought to the past. The one thing NYC is great at is building a future over the past. All had no idea what the future would hold from the past. NYC was growing fast and becoming the place to be. Building was happening all over. We all know the famous skyline that was built during this time.

Brooklyn was also building. A very large High School was being built in 1929. James Madison High School was going to be built on the edge of community called Canarsie. It was on 1906 Bedford Avenue. Of course, it was named after the Native Americans with a small spelling difference. The knowledge of the past ended with the name. As the building was built, the large stone in the front of the school was too big to move. Too expensive to blast. So all decided to incorporate the stone in the front of the building in a garden. Amazingly, no one stopped to notice the numbers on the stone. Nine, six, zero and one were still there etched in the stone for anyone to see. While it was somewhat at the base, no one took the time to see it. I guess when people are working, there is no desire to notice something unique or strange.

The school was built by 1930. The school could hold four thousand kids! This was a new time for kids in NYC. New schools. Huge buildings full of everything a kid could want. Life marched forward. Thousands of kids walked past the garden. The garden was separated from the sidewalk by a six-foot-high black fence. Easy to see through but it provided a barrier to the garden that High School kids just didn't pass. All passed the rock. Some stopped to look at it. Others used it as a meeting point. None noticed the numbers on the other side of the rock facing the school instead of the sidewalk. You would think with thousands of people coming to a school that someone would notice the numbers. No one did and time continued to march on. Custodians blindly pushed lawnmowers past the rock. Once in a while a worker would work near the rock. No one noticed. Time continued to hide whatever the buried stone would hold and what the numbers would mean.

We all have a strong rooted belief on who we are and where we came from. So many of us have a strong attachment to a place or a culture. However, who really knows who we actually are? You see, most of us use our very recent knowledge about who we are. Your grandparents, maybe great grandparents and for most it ends there. However, we are only the most current piece in a long strand. As you go back in time, so many of us are a collection of many cultures and places. We do not like to think about ourselves in this fashion. However, it is as true as the sky is blue. The one constant of humanity is change. We move and fall in love with different people. Maybe not in that order. We get exposed to new foods and get immersed in a new culture and a new identity is born for the next hundred years. Who remembers what we were twelve hundred years ago? On a side note, we might be better off if we all realized that the majority of us are all a bit of everything.

On September 6th 1960, Mannity Guame was born. She was a typical healthy baby in Brooklyn. Her parents were of Spanish descent and the celebration of a welcome new addition was going to be had in the Guame family. Right from the start, Mannity was a strong-willed baby who loved to explore everything in her surroundings. As she grew up in Brooklyn, she attended PS 177 for elementary school, Seth Low Junior High School, and then attended James Madison HS. She had a very happy childhood and would meet many of her friends after school at the "rock" in the front of Madison High School. Many of her friends loved to come to her house for dinner. Her mom was an excellent cook. She created dishes with a twist that created a taste of the past. No one could put their finger on it, all asked but her mom would never tell. So many were just happy to be invited and enjoy the feast she made every night.

Mannity grew up fast and after attending NYU, she got married. Mannity graduated with a degree in archeology. She worked at many of the museums in NYC. She specialized in Native Americans artifacts. She loved her work. Those who knew her always felt she would work for nothing if she had to. She just loved holding onto an object from the past and wondering what it meant or was used for. She had many artifacts in her home. For the average person, they looked like knick-knacks. For her, they were open windows to the past. One day, a day like any other at work for Mannity, she met Manny. Manny Alford was also interested in artifacts. He was an engineer who assembled artifacts into whatever the archeologists wanted him to do. It was love at first artifact. They got married and lived in the now Canarsie section of Brooklyn. They bought a home. 10 East 69 Street was the perfect home for them. It was just built and filled with large spacious rooms. Perfect for two people who loved to have all types of "knick-knacks" in their home. Manny did what all husbands do with "knick-knacks." He asked no questions and just hung, moved and when asked about them always responded that it looked nice. While Manny did recognize some of the pieces he was moving or hanging, he decided not to pay much attention and just get the job done. After all, who wants to spend their day off hanging "knick-knacks." Manny loved baseball and wanted to watch his favorite team, the NY Mets. Mannity and Manny lived in peace and thrived as time moved on.

As they lived their lives, the Alford's decided to expand their family and have a child. Their son was born on a beautiful sunny day on September 6th, 2001. They went back and forth with all the usual names. None were loved by either. As Mannity held her newborn son, she looked out of the window of the hospital and allowed the rays of sunshine to hit her newborn's face. She looked at Manny and said, "How about Ray?" They both loved the moment and Ray Alford was announced to the world.

Ray was a typical young man growing up in Brooklyn. He loved sports, especially baseball. He loved the details of the game. Manny loved coaching Ray. He loved raising a son who loved baseball more than him. They shared much joy on the baseball field together. At times it was tough on all since baseball was always on his mind. Mannity reluctantly agreed to make his bedroom a NY Met themed room. She insisted on placing the usual "knick-knacks" in his room to make it more presentable to her. Ray and his dad always managed to pick only blue and orange colored "knick-knacks" for Ray's room. After all, how can you be an avid Mets fan and not have blue and orange? While the men always believed their mom didn't notice, Mannity always picked those colored "knick-knacks." As usual, Mom was always steps ahead of all!

Ray was an average academic student in school. He did what he had to do so that he could play all the baseball he could. During the winter months he played some basketball. It wasn't his love but winter and baseball just did not work well in NYC.

Ray always felt some pressure from his parents to do better in school. They wanted Ray to maybe march in Mom's or Dad's footsteps. Ray just didn't love or hate school. It just was something he knew he had to do. He always made sure he passed and in the eighty range in his grades. He understood that this was the low end of tolerance that his parents would give him. Ray always made sure he did enough to be in this range. One trait that Ray had that many of his teachers and peers recognized was his honesty and willingness to help others. One day while walking home from school in the fifth-grade, Ray saw a diamond ring on the sidewalk. He picked it up and told no one. Each day he would knock on a few doors where he found the ring and just ask if they might have lost something. Word of mouth traveled about the young boy asking this question. Sure enough, a woman who lived on East 69th Street knocked on the Alford's door. Ray's parents were both proud and angry at the same time. They tried to explain to Ray about the need to tell them, Ray understood but also thought he did the right thing.

In Junior High School, Ray would stand up for a few students who were being picked on for no reason. Ray was not a fighter. However, this did not stop him. Again, he told no one. He would speak to the bullies who sometimes would smack him around. However, Ray did not stop and after sometime, they would stop bullying the kids. The strange part of all of this is that no one knew why the bullies stopped except one teacher. Ray's baseball coach in Seth Low Junior high school knew. Coach Ranascee. He started Seth Low JHS the same time Ray did. At tryouts he told his players he just came here from somewhere else and was just happy to be here to help them become better young men. Coach was one of those people who watched everything. Coach noticed when things changed in the hallway, classes or on the field. Coach did notice that the bullying stopped. He would tell Ray that he knew and would try to thank him. Ray would never say he did anything. Both knew the truth. Both respected each other and let it end there. Ray did all kind of good things but never shared this side of him. It was something that was just inside him. Ray felt that a good deed must be anonymous for it to have any meaning. He rarely shared any of his daily good deeds with anyone.

Strangely, it always seemed like Coach just seemed to know more than he should. As time marched forward, eighth-grade came. Ray was a standout pitcher with a very big leg kick. Many people would come to see Ray pitch. Ray didn't notice but his dad did. Ray blossomed as a young man at Seth Low JHS with Coach Ranascee at his side. Ray looked up to Coach. Coach loved to coach Ray. The team blossomed and did very well ending with a championship in eighth-grade. As the year came to an end, Ray was assigned to attend James Madison HS. He didn't know much about the school. The one thing he did know was that it had a beautiful baseball field and that the team was always good. That was his dream. Strangely enough, Coach was also reassigned to James Madison HS. Their baseball coach retired and Coach was given the job. When the two saw each other in the hallway on the first day of school, they were just overjoyed. Both believed that this was some sort of destiny. Both had to settle in to a new routine in a new school. After all, it was only September. Baseball was far away for the moment. Coach settled into James Madison HS. Each day he walked home. He lived about twenty blocks away on 96 East 10th Street. Coach would walk past the weed filled garden in from of Madison HS. Each day he walked he thought he should do something about it. He decided to start a gardening club. Signs were posted and to

Coaches surprise, a large turnout of about thirty kids came to work and build a garden. It was quite an eclectic group. All types of kids, both sexes and Ray was one of them. How could Ray pass up the chance to be with Coach? Coach was also very happy that Ray joined the club. The club would run two days a week from September to November. Coach and the squad of kids in the gardening club started at one end of the street and weeded, planted, cleaned and designed a garden. The school, community and even the students loved what they were doing and what they built.

Then they reached the rock…

36

The bell for the last period of class, ninth-period, was about to ring. It was a clear sunny day, crisp for October 6th. Ray was actually looking forward to working in the gardening club. He liked the physical aspect of gardening. He also loved the feel of the sun on his face as he was in garden. He was true to his name. The bell rang and Ray with many of his classmates ran out to meet Coach in the garden. Ray's best friend in Madison was Henry. Henry loved baseball like Ray. They were always together. They competed against each other in everything except grades. The race was on to Coach. Of course, it was close and they had their normal funny disagreement about who won. Coach told Henry and Ray to grab some rakes and start to clean all around the big rock. Even as they raked, they created competitions. Who could rake a rock closer to another rock? Who could clean their side faster? They amused themselves on a bright sunny day in October. They decided to take a break and sit on top of the big rock. They were discussing the upcoming baseball season and who would be better. It just never ended. A common friend of both of them was a young girl named Gail. Gail was gardening too. Gail was a whirlwind for them. She had the ability to make fun of both of them at all times. She found their competitions to be silly and quite childish. However, the three of them were always together and they just seemed to be great together. It helped that they shared the same birthday. Parties from grade school made sure they were always going to be together. When you are young, silly things like the date of birth can become a meaningful way to form friendships. They all partied together every year and grew together. Gail hated sports and was the "brainiac" of the group. Ray was always carefree and Henry loved to tweak both of them. A strange collection, but we all know opposites attract. The friendship just worked and they enjoyed each other's company.

As Ray and Henry sat on the rock, Gail noticed and could not help but to start raking around them. Of course, the boys took this as an affront to them sitting on the rock. Gail always knew just how to push their buttons and enjoyed getting under their skin. As she raked and kept circling the big rock, the boys jump down and raked toward her. They reached the back of the stone. When the group clumsily banged into each other as only teenagers could do, the boys laughed but Gail was looking at the big rock and saw what she thought was a ship. The image disappeared quickly as they separated from their silly moment. The boys continued working. They never noticed that Gail was staring at the rock. Young men tend not to be like Sherlock Holmes. The gardening club came to an end and Gail told no one but did keep looking at the rock. Coach recognized that Gail was looking at the big rock. He just smiled.

The three walked home after the gardening club. Henry and Ray were talking sports as usual. They noticed that Gail was not chiming in and making fun of them. Gail wanted to share what she saw but she was nervous that the two "knuckleheads" would just make fun of her. They all went home and had dinner that night. Gail couldn't shake what she had seen. She was dying to tell someone. She wanted to discuss this strange event. She wanted to talk to Henry and Ray together. However, she knew together they would just make fun of her. She decided to talk to

Ray alone. Gail lived on the same street as Ray. Her address was 1 East 69 St. It was a two-family house and Henry's family lived on the second floor. She walked to Ray's house a few doors down and knocked on the door. Ray's mom welcomed her and Ray came running down to see Gail. They decided to go for a walk after dinner. Mannity made a silly comment to both. She just couldn't resist. "Oh, you two are going for a walk." Ray and Gail both yelled at Mannity to stop and they left quickly to let the awkward moment disappear as fast as it came. Mannity just smiled as they left.

Gail asked Ray to take a walk to the school with her. Ray looked at her with the most dumbfounded look. The last place he wanted to go to at 7:00 p.m. was back to Madison HS. She would not listen to him. As they walked Ray picked up a rock and tossed it up and caught it as they were walking. Ray did not notice that Gail wanted to tell him something. After a few blocks of Ray just not paying any attention, Gail grabbed his hand and told him to stop playing with rocks and dreaming of baseball.

Gail said, "I want to tell you something but you cannot make fun of me or share it." She grabbed his hand. Gail never grabbed his hand in all their time together. Ray knew she was serious. He was nervous as hell also. For once, Ray paid close attention to Gail. Gail told him about what she saw at the rock and how it disappeared quickly. Gail told him how she saw something that looked like a ship on the rock. Yet it disappeared quickly. Ray did not know what to say but he now understood why they were going back to Madison. They walked silently to the school. For once, Gail believed that Ray was serious. She felt some comfort that Ray did believe something…

They walked to Madison many times. However, this walk was different for Ray. He was thinking about what Gail said and how he would react if he saw nothing. What would he say or do? Ray stared at his phone and the time just stared back at him. The school was of course empty. Ray and Gail walked into the front garden of the school toward the rock. Ray could not get out of his head that he was with Gail checking out a crazy story she said. Gail grabbed his hand and dragged Ray to the spot she saw the ship. They both stared at the rock for an awkward moment. Ray looked at his phone and the time was 7:31 p.m. Then he looked at the rock again with Gail and he saw it! He saw what appeared to be an old ship and the numbers nine, six, zero and one. Gail saw it too and could tell Ray saw it by the fear etched in his face. A moment later, at 7:32 p.m., they both stopped seeing the image and numbers. Ray new the time because he tried to use his phone to take a picture. However, it left as fast as it came. They both rubbed their hands on the spot they saw the image. They felt nothing but a smooth rock. They were puzzled, worried and a bit nervous. The both decided to sit on the rock. They were both silent and took a few moments to decide what to say to each other. They started to talk about what they saw. They both saw the same thing. Gail got a bit angry at Ray and wanted him to swear that he is not making fun of her. Ray told her he saw it and is scared. They sat there faced each other and said the same sentence at the same time. "What do we do now?"

They both walked home and discussed who do they tell? Of course they wanted to tell Henry. They both laughed at how he would react to them if he didn't see the image. They decided to go to bed and feel out Henry in the morning. When they arrived at East 69 St., they looked at each other with a bit of fear and wished each other a good night sleep. Ray entered his house and ran up to his room. Of course, Mannity laughed as he ran by. Ray jumped into his bed and just stared at some of the knick-knacks his mom put in his room. He wondered why his mom likes these things to begin with. They were always odd looking to Ray. He couldn't sleep and grabbed a curved shaped looking orange and blue stone that his mom liked. It was a shiny stone with a strange brown overtone. A shiny rock in Ray's mind. He grabbed a few of the other knick-knacks. He examined them for the first time in his life. He noticed that each one of the knick-knacks had a number. Nine, six, zero and one on them. He couldn't shake that these numbers matched what he saw on the rock. He decided to talk to his mom. He took the rock and asked his mom, "What are these knick-knacks, Mom?"

His mom told him that they were old Native American artifacts that she had collected over years from working at the museum. His mom grabbed the orange and blue stone out of his hand and told Ray that she found this stone in Brooklyn and the stone was part of a puzzle that she could never solve because she did not have all the pieces. Ray did not ask his mom about the number he saw on it. He asked her if she noticed any writing on the stone. She laughed and said it is the shape and smoothness of the stone that is important. She looked at the stone and told Ray she never saw any writing on it. Ray took the stone and went to bed. He wondered if Gail would see the number that his mom is not seeing? He now had more information than he could process alone. He held the stone in his bed and wondered what part of the puzzle it could be. He knew he needed Gail for this. He wanted to call her but it was late and he did not want to hear his mom laugh at him if he was caught speaking to Gail this night. He decided to try to sleep. As he slept, he had many dreams. After all, we all do. Ray was dreaming about all he saw. His dreams for once turned their attention to all the various knick-knacks in his house. He was trying to assemble a puzzle in his dreams as he slept. When he woke up for school, he knew he had to bring Gail home and they would have to play with all the knick-knacks to see if the puzzle pieces are in his house. For now, Ray got dressed and was getting ready to walk with Gail and see if they would have the courage to tell Henry.

The morning meet with Henry for the walk to school started out as any other. Silliness turned to awkwardness as Gail and Ray went silent as they walked. Henry noticed a bit later than he should have. Gail and Ray tried to defer to each other to start. Ray then stopped at the corner of the school. Gail stopped and Henry turned around and asked, "Why are you two acting so strange? Are you finally admitting that you are dating?"

They both looked at each other and chuckled as Gail grabbed Ray's arm and said, "Yes. We are dating."

Gail kissed Ray. Ray had a surprised look but inwardly he was happy the moment happened. All went to school without telling Henry what they experienced. Ray and Gail decided at lunch they would tell Henry on the way home.

They met after school on the sidewalk outside from the big rock. They started to make jokes about the day. Henry joked about Ray and Gail dating finally. As they got away from the crowds of dismissal, Ray and Gail stopped and told Henry all they have seen and experienced. Henry just stared at the two of them for a moment. He laughed and told them they have been in denial about dating each other so long, that the two of you had to make up a story like this to explain why you two finally got together. You could predict the response Gail was about to give him. Her anger came out and she told Henry this is a serious moment and if he was their real friend he would pay attention and try to have an open mind. Henry changed his tone and told the two of them to prove this to him. The three agreed to go back to Madison at 7:00 p.m. and they would show him. As they were walking Ray told them to hurry up. He remembered that 7:31 p.m. was the time he saw something. He told them they need to get there before this time. Gail expressed some anger at not being told this important piece of information. As they walked rather quickly back to school, they all agreed to share every detail no matter how silly it sounded. Henry was laughing on the inside and was dying to tell them they are crazy. He went along with the group hoping to expose them.

They arrived at the big rock by 7:28 p.m. Ray kept looking at his watch. All three stood in the exact same position in front of the rock. Henry kept asking, "What am I supposed to see?" Ray stared at his watch. They all stared at the rock. A few people who were passing by, took a quizzical look at the three of them. An awkward hello came out from Gail as they walked by. Then as the clock hit 7:31 p.m., all three saw the strange ship and the numbers nine, six, zero and one. Henry screamed liked a baby – "Did you see that? Why did it just appear?" Gail and Ray looked at it but were really relieved that Henry saw it. They also laughed at how scared Henry appeared to be. Ray stared at his phone and as 7:32 p.m. came, they all stopped seeing the image. As they started to walk home, Ray decided he had to share the 7:31 p.m. coincidence. They both couldn't make any sense as to why they see the image and numbers at that time and it disappears at 7:32 p.m. As they were walking, they all decided they had to go to Ray's house and look at the knick-knacks and see if they could figure something out with the nine, six, zero and one.

When they arrived at Ray's house around 8:00 p.m., they went to Ray's room. Mannity brought in a snack for all of them. After all, they were always together and as she left the room, she looked at Ray and smirked. Ray yelled, "Get out, Mom, please!"

Henry teased Ray and Gail a bit. Ray didn't know what to say. Gail saved him and said, "Henry, shut up, I like Ray but let's solve what we came here to try to solve."

Ray was inwardly so happy to hear that but he was so intrigued with what they had to do at the moment. All over Ray's room were some of his mom's knick-knacks. They gathered them all. For the first time in all of their lives, they actually looked and tried to wonder what these things were. As all three of them put the ten knick-knacks on a table, they decided to make sure each of them would examine all ten. Ray would not dare leave his room and take some of the others all over his house. Henry and Gail agreed. They were so worried about what Mannity would think. For now, they had plenty to do. As the scoured each item they did notice that all had one of the numbers – nine, six, zero or one. They decided to group them by number. They tried to figure out if there was a pattern. Ray threw in the 7:31 p.m. issue. After an hour they had more and more questions and even fewer answers. At least, Ray and Gail knew they were not crazy. Henry's confirmation gave them a sense of relief. They all left for their homes around 9:00 p.m.

The next morning the three musketeers woke up and met for the usual walk to Madison like they always did. None of them decided to discuss all they have experienced in the last few days. While that may be strange to us, they were teenagers and they lived moment to moment. Gail and Ray actually held hands as they walked. Henry was the comedian and typical silly teenager. As they reached the school, the three of them noticed that Coach was at the big rock a few yards from where they were standing the night before. The three of them looked at each other as they were approaching the entrance of the school. Coach yelled to the three of them to come meet him at the rock quickly. They looked at each other and walked quickly to the Coach. The twenty-yard walk in the garden to Coach felt like forever for the three of them. They just didn't know what to expect, do or say. Coach asked them what they thought about painting the rock with the school colors of black and yellow? They were relieved but they all said they didn't like it. Coach was taken aback a bit by their uniformity. He looked down and noticed the grass in front of the stone was quite pushed down compared to the rest of the garden. The three of them became tense and could not predict anything he was about to say or notice. The bell rang for the start of class. Coach looked at all three of them with a big smile and said, "Here are some late passes, go to class."

As they walked away he smiled at them and waved as if he knew something. He then sat on the rock and rubbed it eerily with his hand as they rushed away to class. Coach, then walked away with a smile as he went to class also. He did take a look down at the spot in front of the stone. He shook his head a bit and just smiled and went on with his day.

As the school day moved forward, all three were consumed with the strange coincidence meeting they had with Coach this morning. What did he know? Maybe he knew nothing? Could they share what they had seen with him? These thoughts ran over and over in all of their minds. Each stared at the clock in each classroom and all wanted to get out of school and meet to discuss what to do. The last few days have been a whirlwind. Finally, the last class bell rang and as they left school, they met and started to walk home. They would never discuss the strange events until they were a few blocks away and the crowds of dismissal would dissipate a bit.

Ray and Henry were so consumed with all the events that had been going on that they forgot all about baseball tryouts on

October 10th. Today was October 9th. Gail just could not believe that baseball tryouts would jump to the top of the list. The boys told Gail they had to go to the park and at least have a tune up before tryouts. Gail didn't agree but actually gave Ray another kiss and wished him luck. Henry laughed as he teased Ray all the way to the park. Ray and Henry were both skill players. They went through all the baseball drills they knew. Both noticed that they threw, hit and caught balls on a level they never did. They wondered what was going on. Ray actually hit a ball past the three hundred and fifty-foot sign on the field. That was something he never came close to. While the two were practicing, a small crowd of younger kids were watching them. Neither Ray or Henry noticed the show of athletic ability they were putting on. When they finally did notice, both looked at each other, chuckled and for a moment just accepted they seem to be better than they ever were. They both went home very happy with their sudden jump in ability and ready to go to tryouts. Once home, Ray had to call Gail and discuss his new ability. Ray told Gail how he was able to do things he never could do before. Gail jokingly tried to attribute it to her kiss. She wasn't a sports person in anyway and really didn't understand the gifts Ray was trying to say he now had. Gail did bring up the time all three of them were on the Brooklyn Bears little league team. Ray chuckled and as they talked about the end of year little ceramic bear they got. Then they both remembered at the same time. They both yelled into the phone, "Coach!"

They remembered he was their coach way back to little league. Ray was a bit angry and wanted to confront Coach as to why he never brought up he was their coach way back in little league. Ray was six or seven but he was quite adamant about remembering who his coach was. Ray hung up and quickly called

Henry. When Ray asked Henry about the coach of the Brooklyn Bears, Henry paused and yelled on the phone, "Coach!"

All three of them found their little Brooklyn Bear ceramic. They carefully looked at it and on the bottom of each bear was inscribed, nine, six, zero and one. Each felt a shiver run down their spine.

When they met in the morning to walk to school, all three without talking to each other took their Brooklyn Bear with them. They all took them out and saw that the numbers, for Ray they were in red, Henry's was in blue and Gail's were in green. The reality of school hit them. They went to class, put the Brooklyn Bears in their bags while Ray and Henry decided to tryout and deal with this later.

October 10th was bright sunny day. When the last bell rang, Ray and Henry ran out to the baseball field to see if they still have the skills they never had. Coach just arrived at the field when they did. Coach was busy organizing tryouts. Ray and Henry were putting on their spikes and they had a moment to just stare at Coach and both knew he was their coach way back to little league. They were both at a loss to explain why they never have noticed this. They both jumped up, wished each other luck and started to warm up. Gail decided to sit in the stands and watch for a bit. While she didn't understand baseball, the story Ray told her about his ability intrigued her. Besides, she liked Ray and baseball was important to Ray and she wanted to support him in some manner. When Ray noticed her, she smiled at him and Ray smiled back with a confidence he never had. As tryouts began, Ray and Henry did not disappoint. They were the stars of the day. Their abilities were the best they have ever been. Ray was throwing harder and hitting balls farther than ever. Henry was quick as lightening and was fielding balls with the smoothness of a professional. When tryouts were over, the other players actually clapped for the two of them. Coach told all he would post the team tomorrow. Henry and Ray asked if they could speak to Coach privately. He agreed if they agreed to help put away all the equipment. Eventually Gail came down to field as Coach looked up to the stands and made eye contact with her. Coach told them that this was the best he had ever seen them play. They both said they never remember playing like this even in little league. They were hoping for some acknowledgment. Coach asked Gail why she was here today. Gail fumbled for the words but had the courage to take out the Brooklyn Bear ceramic piece from her pocket. Coach grabbed it, laughed a bit and had the biggest smile on his face. The boys were relieved and so impressed at the courage Gail had to try to break the ice without saying anything. Coach looked at the bear and gave it back to Gail and said, "It is great to see that the past holds a meaning for you, Gail."

The three walked home after tryouts. They were discussing so many different things at the same time. Tryouts, the bear statue, knick-knacks and the numbers. They were excited and all believed the Coach knew something. Something he was not telling them. When they reached East 69th Street, they decided to come to Ray's for dinner and really work on the puzzle of the knick-knacks. All gathered at Ray's house around 7:00 p.m. Mannity made a family favorite. Chicken Parmesan with a Native American type rice they all loved. They ignored the spicy broccoli. The discussion at the table turned to the various knick-knacks. Mannity told them that she had been collecting them for years. The museum allowed her to take the artifacts they did not want. She informed them that they were all artifacts from a Native American tribe that no longer exists. The trio never asked Mannity anything about an academic topic so after she responded, Mannity was puzzled and asked them, "What's up here? Why are you three all of a sudden caring about these things?"

They all sat silently. Mannity did not pick up on the loud silence. She just made up a joke about being happy to discuss work with her favorite kids. After dinner, they went to work. They gathered all of the knick-knacks they saw in the house. They were quite stealthy however, Mannity did know they were taking them. She just assumed it was a school project or something. She allowed them their privacy. They grouped them by number again. Looking for any possible puzzles pieces that may go together. No luck. They sat there and stared at all of them. The trio then took out their Brooklyn Bear statues and place them together in the middle of the four piles. They were hoping for inspiration. Mannity peeked in by slightly opening the door. They did not notice her. When 7:31 p.m. came, the three bears appeared to come alive and they moved together and faced the trio. Ray had the state of mind to look at his watch and notice the time again. They stopped moving and remained together. Ray told the group that it is now 7:32 p.m. They reasoned the bears were pointing to something. Ray looked directly across the bears and pointed in the direction they appeared to be aiming at. Nothing was in his room. Gail took out her phone and used the compass app. It was pointing a bit southwest. She brought up a map of the local area and she told them the school was in a direct SW line from Ray's house. They took their bears and made sure to put all of the knick-knacks back. They told Mannity they needed to go for a walk. Mannity knew much more than she let on and told them to have a nice time. They decided to walk to school and go to the garden and just look for something. They were so excited about all that was going on in their lives that they forgot all about where they were walking. They took the long way to school and turned the walk into an hour-long event. When they got there at 8:30 p.m., they searched the garden. They sat on the big rock. They took out their bears and were hoping for some help to make sense out all that has been going on. Nothing happened and they decided to start walking back home. Gail could not accept that they were wrong about the direction the bears were pointing to. She wanted to go back and look again. Ray and Henry were dead set against it. They kept saying that they have checked that garden for clues so many times that there is no reason to look again. As they got to the corner of East 69th Street, Ray looked at his watch. They were about to return to their homes until they all felt the bears moving in their jacket pockets. They all grabbed their bears and placed them in their hands. The bears again aligned themselves in a position as if they were pointing. Ray looked at his watch again and noticed it was 10:01 p.m. Gail was the only one not freaked out. She told them the bears were telling them to go to the school. Gail yelled at the boys that they had to find what the bears wanted them to find at the school. Gail was sure it was in the garden.

40

Gail was the brightest of the bunch. All knew this way back to kindergarten. Gail was just a whiz kid. As she moved from grade to grade, Gail decided to just be who she was and not flaunt it or discuss it. This seemed to help her. She was accepted by Ray and Henry as being the genius. One thing Gail refused to do was to do their homework or help Ray and Henry academically. Way back to fourth-grade she told them they have to do their own work and she would not help them. While Gail had the gift of being a genius, she also had the quality of being a hard worker. A rare combination for most people. She respected the effort she put into everything she did. This was never as clear as their first combined birthday party on June 19th in fifth-grade. The three had grown to be best buddies. Gail decided they would have a party in her backyard. All agreed. Gail worked and made the backyard a perfect event with the theme of summer nights from Grease. That night all of their friends saw firsthand that Gail could work at a project unlike most of them. The party was more than a happy moment. It was the moment all saw that Gail was different from all of them. She was bound for great things. Even the parents were amazed at what a fifth-grade girl could build, create and do in a backyard in Brooklyn. Ray and Henry accepted her for what she was, not a genius or a unique young woman, just a very good friend.

After the bears pointed to the school again, Gail made it clear they were going. Henry and Ray did not dare to say no. They did point out an issue. How were going to get out of the house without explaining something to Ray's parents? Gail peeked out of Ray's room and saw they already went to bed. The three decided to walk fast with the bears. They held the bears in their hands and the bears consistently led them to the big rock in front of the garden at the school. They arrived at the school and went to the big rock. They did what they have been doing for weeks. They searched every spot of the rock. They turned their phone lights on and looked and looked. Nothing was noticed that was not noticed before. Gail was frustrated and sat on the rock. Ray and Henry were telling her they knew this was a waste of time. Gail had an idea. She took the bear and place it on the rock. She told Ray and Henry to do the same thing. The three bears jumped off the rock and landed on the grass right in front of it. They stood up on their hind legs. Ray and Henry were so scared that they lost the ability to think in the moment. Gail kept her composure and tried to notice everything she could. The bears paused for a moment and then dropped down quite hard as if to pounce on a spot. They did this a few times. Gail decided to drop down to the bears level and speak to them. She asked the bears what they were trying to tell her. The bears continued to pounce. One bear seemed to understand that Gail was a bit confused. Ray and Henry were still no help. They just stared at everything and could not manage their fears. The bear walked a bit to Ray. Ray was a few steps from Gail in front of the rock. The bear grabbed the bottom of Ray's pants and tugged it. Gail understood. Something was under Ray's foot. They tried to dig with their hands but the ground was too hard. They all took the bears and went home. They all managed to get back into their beds without any of their parents knowing.

The next day was a day they all would never forget. The past month had been filled with these days. However, all three knew that they had to dig in the spot they tried to dig last night. The walk was filled with thoughts about what they would find. Treasure, poison, maps and all kind of crazy things entered the conversation. Gail had a good time teasing the two of them about how they were scared last night. The boys played it off that they were not scared, they knew to step back and let Gail take the lead. As they approached the school, Coach was standing on the exact spot they tried to dig a bit. A burst of nervous energy ran down their spines. Not fear, just nervousness. They were puzzled at how Coach always seems to be in a spot that they knew. As they walked into the school, Coach just smiled and waved good morning. The bell rang and all three had to put these thoughts aside for a day of school.

When school ended, the three met outside the school for the typical walk home. They looked at the rock and noticed a few shovels were left there. They all thought about the crazy coincidence this was. They decided to walk a bit and wait it out. After about thirty minutes, they returned and saw Coach walking toward the shovels. He saw the three of them and motioned to them to come to the garden and meet him at the rock. After some meaningless small talk, Coach told them how much better they were at baseball. He told Gail how he heard from his colleagues that she may be one of the best students they all have ever taught. The three of them wanted to open up about all that had taken place but Coach's cell phone rang at a perfect moment. He answered it and walked away a bit. The three of them turned to look at the rock and were discussing if they should tell Coach.

They decided they would but when they turned around, he was gone. They looked at the shovels. One shovel was leaning on the rock right on the spot they tried to dig at last night. Amazingly, there was three shovels. This spooked them but they were excited at the chance to get an answer to all that has been happening. Ray took charge and grabbed the shovel. Henry kept looking around to see if anyone was watching them. Gail was looking at each shovel full that Ray tossed to the side. It took about six or seven shovelfuls to hit stone. It was tough to dig up. Gail asked Ray to stop digging a moment. She rubbed off the dirt on the stone as best as she could. She saw the numbers nine, six, zero and one. She paused and told Ray and Henry to look. They knew they found something. Ray and Henry grabbed a shovel and moved the stone. When they pried it up, a rush of smoke came out. It smelled kind of sweet. The bears ripped open each bookbag they were sitting in and walked to the hole and pointed down. Henry kept looking to see if anyone was around. All was clear. The bears stopped moving as they were pointing to the hole. At that time, Mannity was driving by and noticed the three of them in the garden. She honked her horn to say hello and continued driving. Coach came out at this time and walked toward them. The gang managed to grab each bear without Coach noticing. Gail was thinking that Coach knew something. This was too much of a coincidence for her to stomach. When Coach approached them, Gail took out her bear and before she could speak, Coach grabbed it. He stared at it and smiled. He looked at all of them and remembered when he gave it to the three of them. He started to discuss the special skills and traits of a bear. He explained to them why he gave them a bear many years ago. A bear is not only strong and fierce, but also quite intelligent and when a bear senses something, it just doesn't stop until it has an answer. He looked at the three of them and told them that they had these traits when he coached them in little league. All were just stunned. They wanted to ask Coach so many things. They all started to think about the statements the Coach just said. Coach gave the bear back to Gail. A wind blew and the three turned their backs against the wind. When they turned around Coach was gone again! Gail said she was tired of this trick and she would figure it out. However, they turned back to the hole now that the stone was out of it. They saw the strange colored stones. It was covered with dirt. This was not the time to clean it. Ray grabbed it and quickly put it in his pocket. Henry covered up the hole. Gail took a picture of the numbers on the stone covering the strange colored stones. She move the rock to the side with the numbers on the ground side for no one to see. They returned home quickly. They had much to do and figure out.

They rushed home to Ray's house and ran into Ray's room and closed the door quite hard. They were so excited, nervous and somewhat happy that they never even noticed if Ray's parents were home. Manny was. He heard the door slam and smiled. He did not open the door or confront them. He walked toward the door but put his head down right before he reached out to touch the door handle. He then walked away. Henry opened up Ray's bag and grabbed the stones. He took them to the bathroom and washed them. Henry was actually impressed with the beauty of the stone. A brownish-yellow center stone with three larger stones attached to it. The attached stones were blue, red and green. It actually was a quite stunning stone. Gail and Ray waited patiently for Henry to wash the stone. They started to discuss the apparent vanishing act Coach had. They came to a conclusion that they needed to pay attention to this. Maybe they were imagining it? Maybe there was something they needed to discover about Coach also in this bundle of mysteries. Henry came out from the bathroom and was holding the stone. Gail grabbed it from Henry and was also struck by its beauty. Ray stared at it. As Gail was holding it and staring at it, Ray went to his jacket and took out his bear and put it on his desk. A chill ran down all their spines. They didn't know what to do. They wanted the bear to move but it just stood on the desk like the statue they thought it was at one time. Ray now had his chance to hold the stone. Gail sat next to him on the bed and Henry was sitting on a chair.

Henry was nervously talking and Gail actually found Henry's comedic gift to be somewhat soothing when she was nervous. Gail and Henry believed that Ray was always the leader of their group. The past month they have witnessed Ray grow into a strong young man. Ray always thought Gail was the leader since she was the smartest. Henry never gave it much thought either way. However, all recognized that Henry was actually the key to the group. Henry was the comedian and a typical young man. Even when he worried, he wasn't worried, if that makes any sense. Ray held the stone up to the light as it entered his room. Ray looked at his phone. He knew the time was not right. He turned to his two buddies and told them we have to start thinking about the numbers. Nine, six, zero and one. Ray put the stone down. He grabbed both their hands and asked, "What is my address?"

Henry caught on before Gail. Gail was bit perturbed. Henry then asked Gail to state her address. The three of them were shocked at how they missed this. How can the numbers on a stone from the past align with their addresses? While they felt they accomplished something, they realized they just added another riddle. While they were discussing the numbers and their addresses, the three bears moved into a circle and walked right in front of them. While they should have been scared, the bears have become a soothing friend and companion for all of them. Henry looked at the bears and started just stating what he thought a circle of bears could mean. "Could the three bears in a circle mean that we have something in common? Are we linked?"

Gail looked at the bears and jumped up and yelled a bit, "It's our birthday!" Gail turned to the boys and asked them to think about it. "We were all born on September 6th, 2001. The numbers nine, six, zero and one. We have been blind to the clues!"

The bears seemed to have been listening. They started to break the circle and form a line and stand up on their back legs. They wiped their heads as if to mock them that they finally figured something out. The bears then walked back to the desk and returned back to the statues they were. So much time and energy was spent that they all realized they were hungry. Gail and Henry left with their bears and decided to leave the stone with Ray. As they left, Ray asked his dad about dinner. Manny said he was making dinner and it would be in a few minutes. Ray started to talk baseball with his dad. His dad started to discuss that Coach told him you were hitting and playing better than he had ever seen you play. Ray agreed and told his dad he could not put his finger on it but it seemed that he got stronger and better at everything on the baseball field. Mannity just walked in as they were discussing baseball. She rolled her eyes as she always did when they discuss baseball. However, she told Ray that Coach was at the market and also told her that Ray apparently has skills and strength he never had. Mannity took out some of the groceries and told Ray it was her food and cooking that gave him his strength. Manny joked that maybe he could become the next famous NY Met to lead the team back to the World Series! After they all laughed and joked a bit more, Ray did discuss how he could not explain this sudden talent just came out and how Henry had it also. Mannity and Manny looked at each other. Ray thought they would be somewhat freaked out. They were not. Again, he had a strange feeling that they knew something, but he didn't say anything. His dad then discussed that sometimes the stars just come together for a person. You work at something so hard and the stars finally align. Mannity grabbed her favorite knick-knack in the kitchen. It was an old statue of an old Native American tribal leader who was believed to worship the stars. She stared at the statue and told Ray the story she heard about the leader. The leader believed that when the stars aligned in a certain position at a certain time, the universe would pick a person to do or act in a way that the universe needed at the time. Maybe, the stars had finally aligned and given him the gift the Mets needed at this time? Mannity then laughed as Ray and Manny cringed at the words she was saying. They all laughed and had a great dinner. Ray however was thinking and thinking about the story he just heard.

Ray went to his room and laid in his bed holding the stone. He wanted to call Henry and Gail. He looked at his phone and there were many texts to him. He didn't respond or read them. He just wanted some time to process everything and be alone with his thoughts. He actually talked to his bear on the desk as it was just a statue. He asked the bear for help and guidance. He got angry at the bear for not giving more help. The bear remained in statue form. Ray thought about the numbers again. Looked at his watch and saw it was 9:29 p.m. He sat up in his bed with the stone in his hand as he looked at the stars through his bedroom window.

He remembered how 10:01 p.m. was key. Ray kept thinking about the numbers.

He held up the stone to the window as 10:01 p.m. approached. All four stones started to shine brightly. So bright that the light peeked out the sides of his bedroom door. Ray thought his parents had to see it but he was consumed with the moment. It appeared to Ray that the stones were being energized. Ray took a quick look at his bear. It was standing up on his hind legs looking directly at Ray. When 10:02 p.m. arrived, the stones stopped glowing. Ray was not nervous or worried. He actually was so happy that he predicted this. He understood the role of nine, six, zero and one with 10:01 p.m. The bear actually clapped a bit as it returned to statue form. Ray spoke to the bear and actually thanked it for all its help. Ray thought to himself about how much his life had changed. Who would ever believe he would be talking to a statue and actually expecting some kind of response! Ray went back to bed holding the stones. He started to text Henry and Gail about what just happened. Henry and Gail had already texted at 10:01 p.m. that their bears were pointing to Ray's house. As Ray was about to respond he felt some heat from the stones. He examined the stones in the most detailed manner he could. Ray did not have a scientific eye and he kept thinking, a stone is a stone, right? Then why did it shine brightly for a moment? Ray grabbed the rock at the corner of the red stone. He had an eerie feeling as he held the stone and saw his image in the red stone. As Ray watched, the stone dissolved into his hand. He became weak and a bit confused and collapsed on the bed with the stone in his hand. He never had a chance to call his buddies.

The next morning was a school morning. Mannity yelled, "Breakfast in fifteen!" and Ray heard her say good morning to

Henry and Gail. Ray grasped the stone and noticed the red stone was gone. He got dressed as fast as he could and pretended he needed help with his math homework. Gail and Henry understood and joked to Mannity that their duty called. Mannity told them breakfast will be ready for all of them after "their duty". Ray was so excited. He didn't know where to start. Henry picked up the stone and noticed immediately the red stone was missing. Gail saw it also and both were about to yell at Ray until he blurted it all out. He told them every detail. Gail and Henry didn't know what to believe. Ray didn't have any change of appearance in any manner. Henry grabbed the stone and said he would hold the stone tonight. They wanted to believe the story but even this is beyond belief for them. Gail and Henry mumbled to each other, rather loudly, that maybe Ray broke it? Ray was angry at the suggestion and it was dropped immediately. Off to school they went. It was the quietest walk the three of them ever had. When they reached the steps of the school, Gail grabbed Ray's hand and said she believed him. Ray appeared to have needed that and Gail wanted to believe him but her knowledge of the world was being ripped apart every day.

All went to their separate classes. Gail had AP American History. Gail enjoyed academics. Ray and Henry tolerated academics. Gail loved history and actually looked forward to class this morning more than ever. She just wanted to clear her head. As the teacher was discussing the arrival of the Europeans to the new world, Gail opened her laptop and looked up the date. 1609 was the date. Gail had some trouble breathing. She asked to go to the bathroom. The teacher told her to be quick. She went to the bathroom and washed her face. She wrote the year 1609 on the mirror. She moved the numbers around and was shocked! Could this be a key to all that has been going on? She had to return to class. She was eager to hear all about the lesson now. The lesson did not provide any new information. She did look up the year and learned about the local Native American tribes in the NYC area. She knew she had to talk to Mannity. Many times, she blew off a discussion with Mannity about the past. How could she now ask her without her having suspicions? This was a job for Henry!

On the walk home, Ray appeared to just shrug off the disappearance of a red stone into his body. He told his friends that he didn't feel anything different. Besides what else could he do? Tell his parents a stone dissolved into him? That he had a living bear statue? They would lock him up in an asylum! Ray didn't have any plausible explanation. For him, maybe it was all an illusion or dream and the stone was somewhere in his room. Gail told Henry and Ray about her history class. Henry stopped her and told her this is not the time to discuss schoolwork. Gail grabbed both of them and told them about the arrival of the Europeans in this area in 1609. Ray and Henry did not catch on. Gail anticipated this. She took out a piece of paper and showed them that when 1609 was rearranged, it was nine, six, zero and one. The boys stopped. Henry actually said that maybe they need to talk to Mannity about this time. The walk home was now about a plan to talk to Mannity about Native American history without her feeling something was up. Henry told them to leave it to him and just invite all of us over for dinner. Ray took out his phone and called his mom at work. She said it would be great to have the "group" over for dinner. Mannity told all that dinner would be at 6:00 p.m.

Manny and Mannity were a seamless pair in the kitchen. Manny pretended he knew how to cook but the truth was he was only good at cutting and cleaning. Mannity made the favorite meal for "her" tribe. They loved taco night. Henry and Gail knocked and walked right in. After all, this was their home also. Henry started the discussion about his history class and how boring his teacher was talking about the arrival of Europeans in 1609 in the NYC area. Henry went on to discuss that this was why he hated history. It was just so boring.

Henry put on a great show. Mannity bought it. She said she would help Henry and make it so much more interesting after he set the table. Henry turned to Gail and winked. Gail rolled her eyes at him but was happy that they may get the knowledge they need. As all were busy making their version of the best taco, Mannity discussed how a local Native American tribe, the Canarsee, were decimated by the arrival of the Europeans. Her passion came out as she discussed how the new diseases killed almost all of them. She discussed how many of the "knick-knacks" in the house were from the Canarsee. Mannity always felt that the spirit of the Canarsee could be felt in the various artifacts she had in her house. She hated the term "knick-knacks" and used this time to tell all that she called them artifacts and would not allow her family to use that term to describe them any more. Henry jumped in and pretended to admonish all about their lack of respect for the past. Mannity threw some lettuce at him. Henry asked her if any Canarsee survived to this day. Mannity said she did not know. She told them a story she learned by studying the artifacts. The story was about how a Chief and his family died at the same place and legend had it that the spirit of the Canarsee existed in this place. However, no one was ever able to find this place and the story became just that, a story. Henry went on to ask her about the meaning of any of the artifacts in her house. Mannity got up and found a tribal drawing from the Canarsee about a special stone. She kept the drawing in a sealed bag to protect it. She could never figure out what it was or even if it was relevant.

"After all," she said, "it could be a kid's drawing."

She kept it in her house because of the beauty of the picture. The red, green, blue and brownish color was a very pretty looking stone. Mannity gave the plastic bag with the picture of the stone to Henry. Ray and Gail were astonished at this. Henry was all of a sudden charming, polite and not letting on at all about all he knew. Ray and Gail tried to follow Henry's lead in this manner. They were somewhat successful. Manny was busy enjoying his dinner and Mannity was so happy to discuss her job with her "tribe" that she did not notice Gail or Ray's ghostly look as they looked at the drawing. Dinner couldn't end fast enough. They had to leave and discuss all that they have learned. Dessert came and went and somehow, the trio was able to eat and live in the moment. They held the many thoughts they each had to themselves. They helped to clean up as Ray and Gail watched Henry put the cherry on the top of the evening by discussing how much he enjoyed "History by Mannity" instead of his teacher. The group left for a walk.

They couldn't get out fast enough. As soon as they reached a few steps away from the house, Henry let out a, "What are we involved with here? Why us?" Henry took out the stone from his pocket and kept discussing that some kind of magic or voodoo is in stone. No one noticed that Mannity was peeking at them from the front window. They were a bit away. Who knew if Mannity noticed or even saw the stone? Gail became more focused on the entire story. Gail started to discuss how they saw a ship on the rock for a brief moment. She said it made perfect sense that the stone is the embodiment of the lost Canarsee spirit. 1609 fit the numbers that their lives seemed to be linked to.

As Gail continued, Ray stopped them and asked his friends with a bit of fear in his voice, "Then what is in store for me now that the red stone seemed to dissolve into me?"

Both were quiet. Henry broke the scary silence and said he would keep the stones for the night and repeat all the steps that Ray experienced. Ray asked if he could have a sleep over. Both Gail and Henry loved the idea. After all, their friendship was the only thing they had to face all they were embroiled in. Ray went home and quickly packed for the night. This was something Ray and Henry did many times. Ray grabbed his backpack and made sure to put his bear statue in with care. He actually spoke to it as he quickly packed. His inner voice just couldn't shake how all the science he has learned just does not apply to a bear statue that seems to communicate at all the right times. He also found the bear to be a welcome friend during this entire adventure. He tucked it in his bag and left for Henry's. When he got settled in his NY Mets pajama apparel, Ray and Henry started to toss a baseball back and forth. This helped them to discuss things, I guess. As the ball was tossed, Ray made sure to explain that the time is critical. 10:01 p.m. was the time the stones must be held up to the light in the window. It was a clear night again and the moonlight was bright. As the time got closer and closer to 10:01 p.m., both of the boys truly hoped something would happen. Ray for his own sanity and for Henry, a confirmation that he belongs. Ray held his phone and told Henry to get ready. Henry took the stones and as 10:01 approached, he held it up toward the moonlight. When 10:01 p.m. came, all the stones shined brightly again. They watched the green colored stone become a green gas that streaked to Gail's house. In a moment the blue stone was gone also. All they had was the middle brownish stone that held the entire stone together. At 10:02, Ray told Henry this was very different from his experience. The stone got warm and then seemed to dissolve into his hand as Ray held it. Ray grabbed Henry's hand and a puff of blue smoke popped out of his right hand and then went into him. Ray immediately asked Henry if he felt something. Henry didn't feel any different. The two were so focused on what was happening to them that they did not notice their two bears walked over to a desk and pointed to Gail's house. Ray grabbed his phone and called Gail. He told her all that had just taken place. Gail opened her right hand and a greenish smoke popped out and also seemed to have entered her right through her skin. Gail was scared. Ray calmed her down and said all they could do now is sleep and think about the next steps. When Gail put her phone down, sleep was something she could not do. She kept examining her hand. She didn't feel anything. She stared and stared. She was hoping she would notice something. She didn't notice that her bear apparently walked onto her bed on the side of her pillow. The bear pointed to the clock on her nightstand. Gail just didn't notice. Ray and Henry kept tossing the baseball back and forth all night. They couldn't sleep either. They verbalized the idea that they discovered the stone Mannity was talking about. Could the stone have the spirits of the Canarsee in them and now they are in all three of them? Ray changed the subject and told Henry that they may have the varsity baseball season they dreamed of. Maybe the newfound skills came from the stones or the stars or some combination. Both were sure of it and at the same time they were not scared. They both discussed their upcoming dream season and the exploits they would do. All could not sleep. How could any of them? They all kept looking at their hands and examining their bodies waiting for something to happen. Gail had the toughest night. Not only could she not sleep, she didn't have the comfort of having her friend over. She was alone. However, Gail did think deeply about all that just happened to her. She got up close to midnight and looked at the moonlight. Her bear walked to her and as Gail picked her bear up, the bear perched on her shoulder. She felt comfort but could not figure out what the bear was pointing to. Gail turned and looked at her clock. It was 12:01 a.m. Gail opened her hand and as the moonlight hit it, Gail felt a strength she never had. The feeling came and went. The bear climbed down her shoulder and went back to being a statue pointing to her phone. Gail noticed the time was 12:02 a.m. Gail texted both Henry and Ray. They listened but could not understand what Gail claimed she felt. Eventually sleep won and the night past.

Baseball practice was indoors this Saturday. Henry and Ray were in the gym a bit early helping Coach set up for practice. As the team arrived, Ray and Henry started to warm up and throw the ball back forth a bit harder each time. They did not notice that they were throwing to each other quite hard. The sound of the ball hitting their gloves was a sound that was just not normally heard. Their teammates stopped tossing to watch the speed they were throwing to each other with. Henry and Ray did not notice and kept warming up. When they finally did notice, Coach jumped in and said, "Okay, stop showing off that you can throw hard and let's get to work getting better."

    Ray and Henry had the best practice they ever had. While it was indoors, they hit on a level that no high school athlete matched. They were also able to show off their catching skills. Coach asked them to stay after practice and help him clean up as he dismissed the rest of the team. As they were putting away the equipment, Coach asked the boys to think about this newfound ability. The boys told Coach that it just happened. Coach asked them how are they going to use their ability to help the team? They gave the normal answer. The expected answer. However, they felt that the question wasn't about baseball. As they continued to clean up, they wanted to approach Coach about all that happened. As they came out of the storeroom, Coach was gone. They locked the door and left.

The days and months moved to spring. The trio waited for something to change or for them to notice something different. They looked for signs. They even invented scenarios in their mind. Some were quite silly. One morning Henry sat at breakfast sticking a spoon in the peanut butter jar. He was reading his texts from his phone and not really paying attention to anything. He unknowingly dropped his spoon and he could not find it. He searched all around the kitchen table. For a moment, Henry believed the spoon dissolved into him like the stone. As his parents entered the kitchen, they thought he lost something so much more than a spoon. They started to get on their hands and knees to look. Henry abruptly left the breakfast table and ran to his room to call Ray and Gail. As he was explaining all to them, his dog jumped up with the spoon in his mouth. The dog liked peanut butter too. Ray and Gail were also not immune from creating scenarios. One afternoon they were at the library doing their schoolwork. Of course, each had different work to do, unfortunately for Ray. Ray went to get a book and placed it on top of his book bag at the table he was sitting with Gail. Ray went to the bathroom. Gail took the book and placed it back on the shelf and quickly sat down before Ray returned. Ray came back and started playing on his phone. Many minutes later, he reached out for the book and it was not there. He looked around a bit. He also looked under the table in "Henry"-style panic mode. No book. Gail kept working but was laughing inwardly. She then asked him, "What is the problem?"

Ray was nervous but he looked at Gail and started to believe the book just disappeared. Ray created an entire story to prove it. The book was about digestive issues and he just had an issue in the bathroom because the book disappeared. He knew there was a link. Gail played along and allowed Ray to run with this crazy idea. She even pretended to have her own stomach issue suddenly. She asked Ray to walk her to the restroom and as they passed the shelf with the book, she handed it to him and laughed. Ray was not amused at the start but he did come around to see how funny this was in a few moments.

Christmas came and went. They slowly returned to their "normal" routines as winter settled in. They would look at their bears and now find it hard to believe they moved. Henry would look at the stone every night before bed and nothing happened. Ray was a bit different. He was switching to baseball mode. Ray and his dad were going to the cages and actually working out in the local park. They would talk themselves into believing that thirty-eight degrees and sunny with no wind is good baseball weather. For them it was. They played. Ray held back a bit. He did not want to hurt his dad. When they played catch, he made sure to not throw harder than his dad could catch it. His dad kind of sensed this and one day brought it up.

He asked Ray, "How good are you really?"

Ray went out to centerfield. He was at least three hundred feet away. His dad was joking and told him he might as well go back to the house and throw from there. Ray then threw ball after ball to his dad at home plate. Three hundred feet on a line. The throw was so hard that his dad at times stepped aside and let it hit the backstop. Ray was never able to do this. His dad wanted to know how was he able to do this and what strengthening drills was his coach doing? Ray just shrugged it off and said it must be in his genes. They both laughed and just lived in the moment. They were both actually just happy to have this ability as the baseball season approached.

Gail was shopping with her mom on a typical Saturday in February. Food, clothes and then the two of them would go to a nail salon and treat themselves to manicures and pedicures. Gail was close to her mom. Inevitably, the discussion turned to Ray. Gail decided to be honest and tell her mom she liked him a lot and they were very good friends but he is a bit immature at this time. Gail called it the "Henry" effect. Her mom told her that is a trait of all men. Gail discussed her feelings and why she liked Ray. Her mom was just listening and did not grill her. She was so happy that Gail could talk about this with her. The discussion quickly turned to something they forgot to buy at the store. Gail was discussing Ray's favorite drink, soda, and her mom remembered she needed to get some for the week. Some people were coming over. Gail sat back in the chair and could actually see the exact location and words on the bottle in her mind. She tested this gift by thinking about other items in the store. She knew everything. It was as if her mind had the ability to store and recall everything she has seen. She did not tell her mom this at the time. They just went and got what they needed and Gail looked at everything she could to confirm this gift. Gail knew she had something special.

Henry was not to be left out. Henry was happy and while he had his peanut butter moment, he knew he had a gift the same way Ray did. Baseball gave a hint to it. Henry's dad did not like baseball. He actually liked to go to the gym and keep his body in shape as best he could. Many days they would work out together. Henry was always strong and fit. His dad was also. On a day like any other in February, they went to the gym for a workout. Henry noticed how easy the weight was for him in all his exercises. He was very scared to test his strength in such a public place and with his dad. He did it in another way. He went home after a workout and pretended to be sore. His dad told him the usual line, "Drink water and rest a bit before you do anything else."

Henry did. He went to his room and grabbed some forty-five-pound weights. He was able to balance them with one finger. He tested his gift of strength and balancing by tossing the forty-five-pound plate up a few inches on one finger and catching the plate on the next finger. He loved watching the plate dance from finger to finger. Henry, like Ray and Gail, knew he had been given a gift. He didn't know the extent of it or why he was chosen just like the other two. They all shared their stories and tested each other whenever they could. Henry would pass a fork to Gail at a by balancing it on his finger to her. Ray would throw French fries into any object chosen with ease. Gail would tell them about anything she saw with infinite detail. She made sure to use her gift against Ray and Henry by discussing their daily choices of clothing. She pointed out stains, minor rips and how certain styles just do not work together. It was a funny and exciting month as March approached.

Gail also decided to try to get ahead of the events for once. She sat down and tried to play with the numbers and come up with possible dates for some event to occur to them. She multiplied, divided, added and subtracted. She came up with March 1st and March 10th. She decided not to share this with the boys. She wanted to know if she was on to something without any interference or unwanted comments. The snow started to melt away in NYC as March came. March was the time the high school baseball season began. March 1st was a happy day. It was the start of the season. As the three walked to school this morning, all they could talk about was the afternoon of baseball coming.

Gail kept asking them, "What are we supposed to do with our gifts?"

Ray stopped, looked into her eyes and told her she had to start thinking like a baseball player. "Sometimes you have to let the game come to you. You cannot force the moment. You have to wait for the right time, right place and the right moment and it will all come to the three of us. For now, we need to use our gifts in our everyday lives."

Henry and Gail were shocked at the wisdom Ray just let out. Instead of questioning it, they accepted it. Ray kissed Gail as they entered the school and went to their separate classes. Henry pretended to kiss Ray as he went to his class also. Baseball was nine periods away. March 1st was on Gail's mind all day.

As the bell rang for each class, Ray and Henry would pass each other and throw a paper ball back and forth. Tough to do in a crowded hallway. They walked to their next class and kept the maximum distance apart a paper ball can be thrown back and forth. Many kids noticed the skill involved with this and some even gave them a small round of applause. Coach happened to walk by as this was going on. He asked them to stop and walk with him for a few minutes. The hall emptied as the late bell rang. He told the two of them that it was apparent they had received a gift. The boys' jaws just dropped. Coach went on to discuss how the other players on the team had noticed their newfound abilities. He asked Ray and Henry to start teaching the techniques of baseball to their teammates. Coach insisted that they could not win with a team of two. They would have to put aside showing off in practice for a while for the good of the team. Ray and Henry agreed. They wanted to win this year very much. As Ray turned to Henry to shake hands on their new baseball endeavor, they turned to Coach to tell him they would do it. As usual, Coach was not there.

Practice started at 3:00 p.m. promptly. The boys taught and instructed all practice. Ray focused on fielding and Henry on hitting. Coach was actually impressed at how the players were focusing and trying to learn new techniques to get better. Gail hung around in the bleachers doing her homework but was actually pondering if March 1st was going to be an eventful day. Was her math correct? After practice the trio met for the walk home. Gail discussed the significance of the numbers again. Henry and Ray were listening but not really paying attention. They were so excited about baseball. Then it hit Gail! She told Ray and Henry that they were going to be doing homework at Ray's house late tonight. She said she had an idea that had to be tested at 10:01 p.m. Ray and Henry knew that when Gail had an idea, it had to be followed. They agreed and they were actually looking forward to maybe getting an answer to this mystery. After all, each had a stone dissolved into them, living bear statues and a Coach who was a mystery...

Gail and Henry came over around 8:00 p.m. Manny was so excited at the idea of Ray doing homework with his friends. He even prepared them all a snack for the study night. As Manny left, Gail let them in on her number idea. She showed them how she came to the conclusion that March 1st and March 10th would be eventful days. She then told them how 10.01 p.m. would be the moment. Ray and Henry were actually quite relieved that Gail had an idea. They were hopeful that for once, they would start to put this puzzle together in some form. Meanwhile, the bears walked to the side of Gail on the floor and pointed to her. None of them noticed since the bears were on the floor. It was only 9:30 p.m., so they agreed they might as well do some studying. They stopped discussing it and studied. Gail dropped her pen and as she turned to reach it she saw the bears. Henry noticed they were pointing to Gail. All knew they were telling them Gail was right. Each picked up their bear and placed the statue right in front of their computer. As 10:01 p.m. came, they gathered at the window. They looked up at the moon and the stars. They felt this was the right thing to do. A person was walking by. He looked familiar as he continued to walk down the block toward Ray's house. It was Coach. 10:01 came and past. The three sat down and wondered aloud if Coach was the event. They ran outside and met Coach. Questions were flying out to Coach from all three of them at the same time. Coach said, how about you go back and close your front door and we will go for a walk. For some reason all three walked back to the door to close it. They were all worried about what may come. They walked back toward the school. Coach told them about the origin of the stone. How the spirit of the Canarsee was locked into the stone. It was not the fate of the Canarsee to pass away from existence. The stars had a plan for the Canarsee. As the Chief, his wife and their son passed, the spirit of the

Canarsee was placed into the stones. The rock in front of the school was the rock where they passed and the energy entered the stones. As this was explained, they reached the school. Coach told them to walk to the stone. All did. They looked at the stone and all three saw the strange ship and the numbers. Coach smiled since he knew what they saw. They started to walk back to Ray's house. They wanted more answers as the questions poured out. Coach decided to start with the bears. The spirit of the bear was the guardian of the stone.

"The spirit chose the three of you when you were young. The statues I gave you in little league has the protective and friendly spirit of the bear in them. They are your friends and can always be counted on to help guide you."

All three took the bear statues out of their pockets. None of them remembered that they put the bear statues in their pockets. Coach touched Ray's bear with reverence. He spoke to the bear in what appeared to the trio as a Native American language. The bear nodded and returned to lifelessness. They reached the corner of East 69 Street. Coach stopped. They stopped a few steps ahead. He told them that they must trust each other and allow the gifts they received to only be used when needed and for good. "If they are used at any other time, they will not be able to be used." Coach asked the three of them to face each and hold hands. He told them they were forever going to be linked and to trust each other always. They looked at each and as they turned to Coach, he was gone. For once, Henry became the philosopher of the moment. Henry told them he always knew that their friendship was special, and he was relieved to know something. Ray and Gail were a bit more worried. Yes, they had some answers. What were they chosen for? Why them? Gail was inwardly very happy. She figured out March 1st and told Ray and Henry that March 10th would have more answers. Henry and Ray pretended to write on a paper and wondered aloud how nine, six, zero and one was March 10th?

Gail smiled and said, "You should have paid more attention in math class."

All went to bed to think about all that had transpired.

51

The next day worked out to be a perfect day for them. It was some sort of teacher meeting day. The type of day school kids always loved. Teachers had to go to school but not the kids. All three woke up holding their bear statues in bed. They all were looking at it as a welcomed friend and a key part to whatever may come in the future. From now on, they took their bears wherever they would go. As they started texting each other, Gail insisted that they meet at a local park, Marine Park. When they arrived at Marine Park, they decided to find a spot where no one was in ear shot of the conversation they needed to have. Ray started the conversation by taking his bear out of his pocket. He looked at it and wanted to understand why he needed a guide? Henry kept the philosopher spirit alive in him and opened a discussion about being chosen. "Is life a path we control or is it chosen for us? How fair is it for it to be chosen for us? What if we do not like the path that was chosen for us? Can we change it?"

Ray and Henry turned to Gail. They trusted her intelligence. Gail tried to tell them that we need to focus on the events they could understand and maybe possibly predict. According to the numbers, Gail truly believed the next event would happen March 10th. "It is clear we are linked to the Canarsee in some way. Was it a coincidence that Mannity was an expert in the Canarsee tribe?"

Ray kept discussing the many so called "knick-knacks" in his house. He strongly believed that his mom knew something that would help them. It is very hard for teenagers to ask their parents for help in any normal situations. This was far from normal. They decided to come over for dinner and have the discussion. Ray called his mom and she was thrilled to have the gang over. She ended the phone call with a little poke for Ray. She told him she would make sure Gail sits next to him. Ray said the mandatory, "I love you, Mom," in a quite sarcastic tone. Meanwhile, baseball practice was at 2:00 p.m. today. Ray and Henry arrived at practice a bit early. As they were warming up, a few team members came over to them to talk about some of the techniques they were teaching them. Ray continued to show them and told them to keep working on it. The skills take time to master. Henry also chimed in that one day it will just click. Coach arrived at practice and the team jumped into warm-ups and the day of practice. Coach made sure to treat Ray and Henry like the rest of his players. No one suspected that Ray and Henry were special to Coach. Even Ray and Henry at times didn't feel they were special with the team present. Coach was that good. At the end of practice, Coach announced the first scrimmage would be March 10th. As they walked home and texted Gail about the game, Gail sent many "I told you so…" type comments. She also warned them to not try to think about what would come. The baseball game was just part of the process. Besides, dinner was coming with Mannity and Manny.

All arrived and helped Mannity get dinner ready. Manny was even helping. As the table was set, dinner was served. The conversation turned to baseball of course. Gail and Mannity rolled their eyes as they looked at each other. Gail decided to start the conversation and put an end to any baseball talk by stating the three of them have had many strange events happen to them.

Manny and Mannity looked at each other and held hands at the table. Manny said, "It may be the time."

Ray jumped up, "Time for what? You knew?"

Mannity calmly asked them to tell her everything. Henry broke the ice and started the tale from what they saw at the rock. Gail took over and discussed the discovery of the colored stone. Ray then picked it up with the bears. Gail finished with how the stones appeared to have dissolved into them. Then all three in chorus said: "And then there are the numbers."

Mannity took a deep breath and exhaled. She got up and went to another room and brought back a bear statue. She told them she had been working on the Canarsee Native Americans at the museum for her entire life. She didn't know the importance of the bear statue. Manny has been piecing together many of the incomplete artifacts we have discovered. The curator of the museum has always allowed us to work on this project for our entire working life. We found it strange that he has allowed this since we have never placed an exhibit about the Canarsee in the museum. We didn't question it. Mannity then said, "As we discussed before, no one knew the location of the colored stones. All the evidence we had pointed to their existence. We just couldn't figure out where it was. Coach came over one night and told us that you three are the chosen ones. You would discover the stones and begin to fulfill a destiny that was set in the stars from the moment the Europeans arrived and the death of the Canarsee started in 1609. We didn't understand any more than you do. However, we learned to trust Coach. He always seemed to know and was always working for the greater plan."

Manny then asked, "What special abilities have each of you noticed?"

Henry started to discuss that his strength was way above

normal. Ray discussed how he was stronger also but his coordination was just off the charts. Ray had to show off by throwing his plate of food up in the air and catching it without a morsel of food dropping on the top of his pinky. All turned to Gail. Gail told them that whatever she read or viewed, she had a complete memory of. She grabbed the bottle of soda and quickly read the ingredients. Turned the bottle and read the ingredients aloud in the order they were written with an amazing ease. She then added that many of Ray's clothes had small stains and he needed a makeover. Henry agreed. Mannity agreed also. Manny went to the living room and grabbed a model of the stone he had created. It looked exactly like the stone they found. Henry told them he only had the brownish-yellow stone in his room. Mannity wondered aloud about the role of the remaining stone.

"Is it looking for a fourth person?" All the research she had done had never explained the reason for the fourth stone. Ray said the red stone dissolved into him. Mannity said that was the Chief's stone from the legend. Henry said the blue dissolved into him. Manny said that was the son's stone. Gail jumped in and said the green dissolved into her.

She added, "Let me guess, that was the Chief's wife?"

Mannity nodded in agreement. Manny stood up and said, "We now have to figure out why you three." Mannity always felt Coach knew the answer. Manny picked up the phone and invited Coach to dinner tomorrow. He gladly accepted.

The next day was far from a normal Saturday. All could not wait for dinner with Coach. Ray and Gail decided to show Mannity and Manny their bears and hoped they would move and react. Manny instantly recognized the statues as their little league gift. Gail told all that it was 10:00 a.m. and they were hoping at 10:01

a.m. they would move. As the correct time came, the bears did not disappoint. They walked to Mannity and rubbed her leg with what appeared to be gratitude. Manny yelled that it all made some sense to him now. Right on time at 10:02 they stopped moving and pointed toward Henry's house. No one made any sense of this in the moment. They were all excited about understanding the role of the bear. So many of the artifacts in the house had bear like looks that they were relieved to know. Ray told them what Coach told them about the bears. Mannity and Manny smiled at Ray and Gail and told them that great things were in store for all of you. They all were going to ask everything they could when Coach arrived later.

Coach rang the bell promptly at 6:00 p.m. Henry ran to the door and welcomed him in. Coach was then welcomed by all. They sat the table. The dinner was already prepared and set on the table. Coach decided to help himself first. He told them all he knew why he was there. He asked if they could eat first and talk about the day. They agreed. As the meal came to its end, Coach decided to start discussing the bears. He told them how the bears were given to him by his coach. He was told thirty-five years ago that the bears would guide him and eventually let him know who they should go to. Coach just decided to believe this and he followed the guidance of the bears.

"When the bears chose you three, I knew you three were chosen to fulfill a role." Coach stressed how he did not know what role. Mannity jumped in and asked about the stones. Coach stated the obvious that the spirit of the Canarsee Chief, Chieftess and Mamalis was in the stones and now in each of them. Coach stood up and looked out a window at the evening stars. He told them that all have a role to play. "We do not know our role until we do it. In the end, we each must do our part for the plan that the stars have set for us to occur." He reached out and the three bears came to Coach. Coach went on to explain that he did not understand the special gifts that the bears had. He turned to Mannity and said, "You probably could find the answers. You have more knowledge about the Canarsee past than I." Mannity was puzzled because she did not know at the moment. Coach then turned to the trio. He looked at his watch and said it's 9:00 p.m. "I must be getting home. Before I leave, I want the three of you to understand that you have a great path to follow. I do not know the details nor the ending. I am just a small star among many in the sky. You three have been chosen for a reason I do not know nor do I question."

The bears stood up on their hind legs again and clapped. Before Coach left, he said. "We must live our lives in the time we have been given. I will see all of you Monday at school and then baseball practice in the afternoon." He then turned to Gail and said, "You are the one who must guide them." Coach said goodbye and thanked Manny and Mannity for a great meal and left. They went home with more answers than they had ever in this saga.

Monday came and during the morning walk to school, Gail showed Ray and Henry how she came to the conclusion March 10th was the date for something to happen. Ray and Henry accepted her logic. They could not refute her math. Henry then asked her what she thought would happen? She didn't know and Henry knew that. He just asked to get confirmation from her. The week passed by like all school weeks do. Then, March 10th arrived. The walk to school was now about meeting at Gail's house for dinner, schoolwork and hopefully more answers. Henry and Ray came over around 7:00 p.m. The trio had so much anticipation that every minute seemed like an eternity. They went to Gail's room and pretended to study. Who could study under these circumstances? Only Gail could. They watched the speed at which she was turning pages on her laptop. They were beyond impressed. Henry told her she just read more pages in this short time than he did in his entire life. Gail responded that it showed. Gail's mom was a big Mariah Carey fan and she was playing her hits. As 10:00 p.m. came, they heard her playing her hit, Vision of Love. Henry took out the remaining stone from his pocket. Henry thought that maybe a vision could come from the stone. At 10:01 p.m. in an unplanned moment, Ray and Gail reached for the stone and all three had touched the stone at 10:01 p.m. The three started to see the spirits of the Chief, Chieftess and Mamalis enter the stones that dissolved into them. A fourth person appeared to them and told them that the greatness of the Canarsee would be restored with them. This person also told them that the journey would be a life-long endeavor ending with the Canarsee taking its rightful place in the new world. It appeared to the trio to be longer than a minute however when 10:02 p.m. came, the vision was over. However, Gail's mom was in rare form singing the end of Vision of Love. Ray talked about he was tired of never really getting any answers. Just one continuous riddle. Henry felt that they had the answer and the key was to live their lives and allow whatever role they had to play to occur when it comes. Gail just listened and refrained from commenting. This drove the boys nuts. They needed her to give them her wisdom at moments like this. Gail just didn't have any wisdom in this moment.

The next day at baseball practice, Coach informed the team of their schedule, and the first game would be tomorrow. After practice, Henry tried to explain to Coach what took place last night. Coach listened but told Henry he must live his life and allow whatever comes to be at the proper time. To think about the future without knowing anything would be fruitless. Henry understood. Ray jumped in and discussed how he could not wait for the season to begin! The next day was all Ray and Henry hoped for. They were stars in the field and in the batter's box. For the entire season, they were the talk of the high school baseball community. Manny was living a parent's dream watching Ray. As the season approached its end, Madison made the championship, which was to be played at Citi Field, home of the NY Mets! Mannity couldn't tell who was more excited, Henry, Ray or Manny. Coach seemed to take it all in stride as if he expected this to happen. The game was to be played on June 20th. Gail had told Coach that June 19th at 11:36 p.m. would be the next time something would happen. Coach wrote that date down on the bottom of the bat he used for practice. After practice on June 19th, Gail came to Coach to meet Ray and Henry. She grabbed Coach's bat and asked him to look at the date on the bottom of the bat handle. He told Gail, he had no need to. Coach told her that he had complete faith in her and she never had a need to prove anything to him. Ray and Henry grabbed the bat and saw the date. They turned to Gail and asked again if she knew what may come. She didn't but she knew the next step in the journey would be tonight at 11:36 p.m. They could not be together for this so they all agreed to have their phones charged and ready. As 10:00 p.m. approached June 19th, Ray and Henry texted Gail why she believed 11:36 p.m. would be the time instead of 10:01 p.m.? Gail said it was all in the numbers. They pretended to know by texting the blah okay. Henry and Ray texted each other and kept wishing they could figure this out for once before her. For the next few hours, the theme of the texts was a lot of guessing about what may happen. All had their bears in full sight during this time. At 11:30 p.m., Ray decided to call Gail. He was nervous about what their future could be. Ray asked Gail about the possibility of them being used by this "spirit" for something they didn't feel was right. Gail agreed that this was a real worry. However, nothing that had happened had even remotely leaned toward anything bad. Gail had a feeling that tonight they would learn about the future in some way. As they hung up, the bears walked to all of them and sat next to them looking up. When 11:36 p.m. came on June 19th, all three were looking up in the direction of the night sky. They all saw the exact same story. It wasn't a dream since all were awake. It was as if the stars became a viewing screen for a moment for them. It sounded as if it was narrated by someone who they actually understood. The story was about three young people who embodied all that the Canarsee held dear who were casted into the future. In that future, the three would face many obstacles that they would overcome to build a great Canarsee nation. This nation would show the people another path. A more peaceful and loving path. At the end, all three were given a look at the three people in the story. They did not appear to look like the three of them. They appeared to be Native American in appearance. When the story ended, all three went to sleep immediately. The bears rolled over next to each of them as if they went to sleep also. In the morning each felt that it wasn't a dream but more like a movie they were allowed to watch.

Ray decided to tell his parents all about this in the morning. Mannity listened with a very trained ear and eye to every detail. So did Manny. Mannity wondered aloud if this was a hint that the three of them had Canarsee blood in your genes. Mannity wondered about her past also. She decided to put science to work. Manny and Mannity with the trio decided to have their DNA examined for indigenous American populations. It was an autosomal test. Mannity warned that this could not tell them any specific tribe but it could tell with complete accuracy if they had that line of ancestry. Mannity called someone at the museum and a quick train ride to NYC and the test was taken. The results took about a month to obtain. They did all they could do. Once home, Mannity and Manny gave serious thought about linking to the Canarsee. They came up with a very unique idea. Many of the Canarsee artifacts in the museum had not been touched by anyone without gloves. Mannity asked Manny if they went to the museum, could they choose some pieces that would yield some DNA from the Canarsee? Manny thought the idea could work. They set to work on choosing the right pieces and the next day had them sent to the lab to see if any DNA could be tested. Meanwhile, Ray and Henry forgot all about the baseball championship game and they had to meet the team at 4:00 p.m. to go to Citi Field. They somehow managed to put all this aside and focus on their dream of winning the championship. That night at Citi Field, they performed like stars and Madison won the city championship. Ray and Henry were the talk of the baseball recruiters in the stadium. School ended a few days later. Coach told Ray and Henry he would see them all summer at baseball camp. Gail was ready to have school out of the way to help figure out the future that was in store for all of them.

69

The first day of summer for a high school kid is magical. School is a multi-faceted emotional wheel. Young people always say they hate it but they also love it. If school was a wheel the spokes would be more than just education. Social events, sports, clubs, hanging out and just plain silliness would also be spokes on the wheel. When school ends, the wheel changes. Different friendships and times exist in the summer, and they are very different from school life. The first day of summer for Gail was a pen and paper event, to figure out the dates that may matter. She came up with July 9th and September 6th. Her and Ray decided they would spend a day at the beach at Coney Island. After they set-up their towels and preparations for a great beach day, Gail asked Ray what he thought about his freshman year and all he accomplished. Ray let his guard down and told her that he was living a dream. He started with his newfound courage to speak to a beautiful girl and date her. He added with a bit of sarcasm how his grades had never been better. He actually admitted reluctantly that he was proud of his newfound academic success. Being the star as a freshman on a team winning the city championship in baseball was beyond his wildest expectations. He then paused and said to Gail, sometimes he felt he was being tested by a greater force. Gail agreed and told Ray how she became the academic star of her class. They both discussed Henry's gifts with silly Henry stories. As they laughed and enjoyed the sun, Gail took pleasure in not sharing how she figured these dates out. Eventually, the relief of no school and a beautiful summer day at the beach won the conversation.

Henry decided to spend his first day of summer at the park playing baseball. Many of the kids who attended different schools met in the park for a pick-up game. The baseball community for NYC high schools was a very friendly one. Henry enjoyed all of the attention from his peers asking him about his newfound strength and ability. The jokes of steroids abounded. Henry told them all that it was just hard work and dedication and one day it all came together. As the game started, Henry was in centerfield. He would look up to the sun and have a conversation in his mind with the sun. He kept asking why he had this ability and what was it ultimately for? Of course, he never had a response. Luckily, he was in centerfield far from others, at times he wondered out loud what he would do if he ever received a response to the questions he was mentally asking. As the game progressed and Henry's abilities shined brighter than the sun on the first day of summer, Coach was just walking by. He stopped to watch the game and waved to Henry in centerfield. When the inning was over, Henry came over and sat next to Coach in the stands. Henry asked Coach what he thought of all that has transpired.

Coach turned the question around and asked Henry, "Why do you believe you were given these gifts?"

Both were quiet for a moment. Henry then responded that he believed he was part of a bigger plan and the gifts were just a tool for the plan to happen.

Coach agreed and then asked Henry, "Why do you believe that I know more than you?" Coach went on to tell Henry how proud he was watching Henry handle his gifts in a very professional and respectful manner. Coach said he was worried that the gifts would change him. Henry jumped in and said the gifts had changed him. He had never been as introspective about things the way he is now. Coach shook his hand and told him to "live his path." Henry was due to hit and Coach was gone as always when Henry turned around to say goodbye right before he entered the batter's box. Henry just smiled and proceeded to hit a double.

One beautiful summer day rolled into another. The trio managed to stay together each day for something. Each day they discussed what they hoped for July 9th. They all agreed that they wanted something that may never come. What did the future hold for them? Why them? Did they have free will or was their future set in stone? Big questions for sophomores in high school. They actually made fun of themselves for these questions and discussed how they have all changed so radically over the past year. The morning of July 9th came. All three decided a day at the beach and the rides at Coney Island was the choice for the day. As the morning rolled into the afternoon, the trio noticed Coach was walking by. They yelled to him and he came over. He sat in the sand with them and stared at the group. It was awkward for the trio but not Coach. He had a huge smile on his face as he looked at each of them. He told Gail she was correct again about the dates. Coach looked at his watch and asked Gail if she knew the time. Gail smiled and told him it was 3:01 p.m. Coach didn't look at his watch and told her she was right on as always. Henry and Ray were lost in the moment. Coach asked them what did they see when they looked up at the sun? None answered. Coach went on to ask all if they believed everything was just an accident or was there a force or will that made sense out of the chaos? Gail started to answer but Coach stopped her. He discussed that the answer doesn't matter. Either way, paths are created for all. If someone doesn't measure up to the chosen path, other paths are then taken. Coach told them the remaining stone that was created a long time ago, was the start of their paths. "The stone chose you three because of the numbers, the past and the way you have handled your gifts. The next three years will be filled with paths. You must "live your paths to the best of your abilities."

Coach asked Henry to look in his beach bag for the stone. Henry told Coach it was not there. He looked anyway and his bear pushed up the stone to Henry. Henry in amazement, grabbed the stone and handed it to Coach. Coach grabbed the stone and held it in his hand. He allowed the sunlight to hit the stone. Three rays of light jumped out of the stone and hit each of them. Coach smiled. He said a path was set long ago by a very wise man. "The three of you are on the path to do great things but you must 'live your paths' in a manner that is worthy of the paths chosen for each of you." Coach reminded them that they were not superheroes. This was not a super-hero event. They had been chosen to help people and restore the Canarsee name to the present. Coach handed the stone back to Henry. He told him to keep better track of it since he would need it someday. This time Coach walked toward the sun. As they said goodbye, the light was too bright to see him for a moment. All three rubbed their eyes and looked quickly for Coach. He was gone.

The summer was a perfect summer for them. They settled back into normal teenage life. They lived their perfect summer lives and somehow managed to put all that had happened to them in the back of their minds. Even Manny and Mannity put it out of their minds. They enjoyed watching their "little boy" grow and mature into a fine young man. Sophomore year came for the group with some anticipation as September 6th approached. This time, the date came and went like any other day. The next three years of high school were as normal as they could be for three young people endowed with special gifts. Henry and Ray won city championship after city championship in baseball. Gail became the valedictorian of her class. Henry and Ray were no slouches with their grades also. While they kept waiting for something to happen, nothing did. It was as if they were allowed to return to their normal lives and grow into their gifts. As the senior year started to melt away, April came with the notices of college acceptances. They agreed to try to attend the same school so they could face whatever their paths were together. The school they all wanted to go to was NYU. Easy for Gail and a bit of a reach for Henry and Ray. The day came and all three were accepted. The families went out to celebrate and at dinner the unfortunate reality of the large tuition settled in. How would they pay for it? All the parents stated that they could not afford the fifty thousand dollars plus tuition without help. Mannity somehow remained calm and told them to trust the path they were on and let it play out. A week later they all received their financial aid packages. They decided to not open the email in front of anyone other than themselves. They walked back to school and sat on the rock where this all started. Gail was pressured to open her email first because they felt she would get the best aid package since she was the smartest. She told her "two men" that it was nice to finally hear it. She sat on the rock and opened the email. She held her breath as she read the email. She received a full academic scholarship. Henry decided to open his email next. He pushed Gail off the rock and told her he needed the help from the rock more than her. Gail smiled and agreed. Henry sat on it as Ray and Gail held hands. Henry read the email out loud. He received a full baseball scholarship! He didn't even finish reading the email. He jumped up and embraced his two best friends. Ray then sat on the rock and was very nervous. Gail put her arm around him and told him to trust his path. Henry was nervous. He could not envision life without his best friend. Ray opened the email and kept a sad face. Gail and Henry froze with worry. Ray kept reading the email and could not keep up the joke. He jumped off the rock with a smile and read the email out loud stating he received a full baseball scholarship also! As the three were jumping and hugging, Coach walked by with an NYU baseball t-shirt on. The three ran out to the sidewalk and walked with Coach. They took a strong tone with Coach. They wanted to know how he knew. Coach informed them he applied to be the head coach of NYU baseball. He was given the job in March. They were so happy to be together. Coach could not resist poking Gail about the date. He asked her if her math skills over the past few years had gone soft? Gail stared at him with a puzzling look.

Coach said, "The date is April 9th correct? Did you think the numbers have left you?"

Gail smiled. She figured it out and hugged Coach. Henry wanted to know if the journey would start again? Coach continued to stress the need to follow their paths with the best of their abilities. All three nodded and the next two months were fantastic. Prom, graduation and a summer knowing they were all going to NYU for free. At the end of summer, they packed for their dorms. Of course, Henry and Ray shared a dorm. Gail was a floor below. She lucked out and somehow got the only single dorm room a freshman could get. Her dorm was a small palace. All three prepared for their new lives and were just so happy.

Freshman year started and each found their niche rather quickly. Henry and Ray took the normal freshman courses and both fell in love with the idea of being lawyers. They themselves were actually shocked at how well they were doing in their classes. Fall ball started on the group's birthday, September 6th. On the field with Coach on a baseball scholarship still seemed surreal for them. Right from the start, it was clear Ray and Henry were the stars of the team. Coach decided to continue what had worked for him. He used Ray and Henry as tools for all. Both young men were a bit uncomfortable leading drills. They followed what they were asked to do and their teammates did accept them willingly. After all, talent does shine and people tend to notice talent very quickly. Gail took a different path yet the same idea of talent rising to the top occurred for her. Gail took the usual freshman classes also but added an archaeology class in Native Americans. The Professor recognized Gail's academic gifts. The Professor also took the time to help develop the gift she saw by asking Gail to work with her on her current project. Gail jumped at the chance. The idea of working with Professor Fiao as a freshman was such an honor. She was world renown expert on Native American tribes. She was working on a possible discovery that was located under one of the buildings in downtown Manhattan. After all, NYU owns most of lower Manhattan and she was lucky enough to trace a string of evidence that led to a dig in the basement of the building at 1690 Madison Street. NYU owned the building and agreed with her about the possible importance of the site. The numbers and the address of the site was not lost on Gail. Neither was the Professor's last name. The nickname of the building even had intrigue for Gail. It was the Longhouse building. That night they all met in Gail's dorm to celebrate. They shared all their successes and discussed every possible avenue when Gail told them about her news. Henry actually turned a shade of white when he heard the address of the dig. Gail had a great time pointing out that they finally recognized the "numbers." Henry and Ray were so nervous that Gail told her new Professor everything. She assured them she did not. The bears even came out to celebrate and walked to the window while this conversation was going on. They pointed toward the address. Gail knew this quickly. She could see the direction of the building from her window. Gail had a strong feeling that the future of the three of them was tied into that dig. She had no idea what the discovery would be but she knew the future of all of them was at the bottom of the building.

The spring semester rolled on and Ray and Henry dove deeper into their academic career. They took more classes with a legal tilt. They were both so surprised how much they loved the law. When they discussed the law with each other in Gail's dorm, Gail was amazed at the raw academic passion they both displayed. She would even point out how she believed they had more passion for the law than baseball. The young men would never admit it but they thought about it. Ray would always rescue the moment by telling Gail the most passion he had was for her. Henry would second the idea and the young men would be saved from admitting law inspired them more than baseball. The spring semester started on all cylinders for Ray and Henry. They were the stars of NYU on their first college baseball trip. Every day they were celebrated on the NYU athletic website for something they did on the baseball field. NYU was even starting to be noticed on the college baseball scene. During all this athletic glory and small amount of fame, Ray and Henry always made time for studying and discussing law. During a game Ray even yelled out to Henry in centerfield an answer they were debating before the game. No one knew what they were talking about, and it was laughed at since Henry made a diving catch right after Ray's comment to him. Gail was doing more than great. She was showing all her peers that she was quite gifted. All her free time was spent at the dig. Professor Fiao loved that Gail was working at the dig and loved the chance to train and teach someone so gifted and passionate about the past. The Professor took Gail into a clean room at the dig. The clean room was a room with the discoveries and artifacts that have led to the dig. It also contained all that was discovered at the dig. Gail had been learning the skills required to work at the dig and was never told what they were digging for. She searched the internet and the past books written by the professor but she could not discover what may be under the building. However, Gail did notice the location of the building would have been near the shore during the year 1609. She also took the time to research the current address and place it on maps from that time. She saw that it was possible for the Canarsee to have landed or paddled by in their canoes. Gail even took a day to have lunch with Mannity to discuss this. Mannity was so proud of Gail having the opportunity to work with someone so distinguished. Mannity told Gail that many of the artifacts she worked with in the museum came from Professor Fiao. Mannity never had the pleasure of working with her directly but the two had communicated by email. Gail asked Mannity if she believed something could be at the dig to explain all that has happened. Mannity also sneaked in a question about how her relationship with Ray was going. Gail was no longer embarrassed to discuss her relationship with Ray. She told Mannity how the two of them get along great. She added that Ray had been an emotional rock during all that had happened.

Mannity was very happy to hear it as she put her cup of water down. She then had a moment of clarity. She told Gail they had to go to her house immediately. Once they arrived at her house, Mannity ran into her bedroom and found a series of cups. She put them together and it was a picture. Not the clearest of pictures. It was a picture of a Chief receiving a box from someone in the colony with a high-ranking member of the tribe behind the Chief.

Mannity told Gail how she never thought about the cups revealing a special moment. Gail wondered if the story on the cups was what they were looking to be discovered at the dig. When Gail returned to the dig, she entered the clean room. She made sure to stop herself from touching anything. She saw two of the three cups Mannity had in her house. She did not want to upstage the Professor in any manner. She did have the courage to finally ask the Professor what the goal of the dig was. The Professor smiled and told Gail she wondered when Gail was going to ask. The Professor told Gail she attended a lecture in London a few years ago. It was not a normal invitation. NYU Brass was very nervous about a "possible situation" arising and they needed her expertise at this lecture and give them her thoughts. The Professor in London was discussing a story he stated he had evidence about. The Professor discussed how many of the Dutch settlers in so called New Amsterdam were very upset about taking land from the people who were there before them. The lecture continued about how one member was elected to be the Governor of New Amsterdam. He was recognized as the leader for only one day. Many of the Canarsee were starting to suffer and die from the diseases the Europeans brought. They wanted to relocate and return the land to the Canarsee. They wanted a place far away from any native people. This "consciousness" was anticipated in the Netherlands. They sent a ship about a month or two after the first ship with explicit directions about who was to be in charge. Gail then wondered aloud if the story ended and how this led to her being in a clean room with someone so distinguished. Professor Fiao paused and just stared at Gail. Gail felt very uneasy at the moment. The Professor then walked around and locked the door on the inside and shut off the cameras in the clean room. The Professor then told Gail that the story ended there at the lecture. That night she received a dinner invitation from the Professor giving the lecture. The story continued at dinner. The governor for the day gave the Chief of the Canarsee Tribe a deed to all the land of the island they were on. In return, the Governor asked for time to resettle in a different place that the Canarsee would help locate. The Chief depended on his medicine man. One of his many gifts was his ability to learn languages quickly. Professor Fiao wondered aloud how the Chief could communicate and understand such a transaction? The Professor went on to explain to her that the Canarsee were watching the Dutch from canoes. The medicine man probably learned the language from listening from his canoe. The deal was explained to the Chief by the medicine man. The Chief agreed by allowing his medicine man to put his fingerprint on the paper. The paper was then sealed in a very small, locked container and given to the Chief. The Chief never took the box with the deed inside it. He let his medicine man take it. He supposedly asked the Chief if he could stop on the banks and enact a spell on the box. He was given permission. The curse made the deed not visible to anyone not worthy of reading it. Professor Fiao then told Gail the end of the story was the issue.

"We have records of what the second ship sent. It stated who was to be in charge when the ship arrived. It never stated that the election of the so called "Governor for a day," was invalid. Now here is the real worrisome part. The deed contained a forever no sale clause. The Dutch must abide by the agreement and vacate the island by the end of the year and never return or enter into any bargains for the ownership of the island." Professor Fiao then paused a moment. She then went into a what if scenario. "This agreement would mean the Dutch could never purchase the island from the Canarsee. The land was eventually given to England by various treaties. How could they give the land to England if they did not own it? Imagine how sticky this would be in a court of law today? The deed or treaty was never found nor ever mentioned during history until I found certain artifacts in the basement of this building. Once I found these artifacts, the brass at NYU have been very supportive of my work. I think you understand why now."

Gail had to tell Professor Fiao how Mannity had the three cups. When she did, the Professor emailed Mannity and asked if she could come over to get them. Mannity responded and the cups were sent to the clean room. Over these few days, Gail continued her work at the dig. She stopped the Professor one day and asked her the question she had on her mind since she heard the entire story. "Are we looking for the treaty at this dig?"

The Professor smiled and said with all the authority she had, "Yes!"

As the freshman year ended, Ray and Henry became the baseball stars of the college world. NYU won its first ever college world series! Henry also impressed his professors and was invited to intern at a law firm. Henry asked if Ray could join him and the Professor was delighted to help the two young stars on the field become stars in a courtroom. Ray and Henry dove into learning the art of researching legal topics. Henry actually loved researching and learning the law. Ray took a more academic view of this as something he had to learn to reach his goal. The two found that being stars on the baseball field seemed to open many legal doors for them. After a half day of researching on a beautiful summer day, they were allowed to leave early. They decided to go to the beach and just relax. Coney Island was only an hour away on the train. They hustled and made it there by mid-afternoon. Once at the beach, Coach just happened to be walking by. This time, the Coach noticed his stars laying in the sun. He called over to them and they waved to him to come over. Coach talked about all the joy they gave him over the past ten years. He also was very proud of the internship they had. Coach actually decided to let more emotion out than he normally does.

He told each of them, "The stars picked wisely with you two. You have not allowed your athletic gifts to overwhelm you or change you in any manner. The two of you are fine young men who will follow a great path and do great things."

Ray and Henry were not used to Coach being so emotional. They decided to take advantage of this moment. Ray asked the Coach to please give them more information about this so-called path they were navigating. Henry nodded in agreement. Coach looked up at the sky on this beautiful day and turned to his stars and said he would give them all they wanted. He stood up and said he had to go but the answers they wanted were easy to get. He told them to go see Gail. They looked at each other and when they turned Coach was gone. Relaxing at the beach was over. They cleaned up, hopped on a train and met Gail at Madison Street. The three walked around lower Manhattan as Gail told them all she now knew. Ray actually remembered the cups in his parent's bedroom.

Henry stopped and looked at his two best friends and just

asked, "Is this our path? Why do we have these athletic skills then?"

Gail agreed that her gift made sense but the athletic gift doesn't make sense. When Gail found out that they saw Coach at the beach and he told them, she wondered aloud how he always seemed to know much more than he should.

Coach decided it was time for him to take a larger role in the lives of his special group. He walked by the building on Madison avenue and "bumped" into Professor Fiao. She noticed his NYU baseball shirt and asked him if his kid was on the team. He told her that he was the Coach. She congratulated him about his recent championship and continued to have a conversation about the team. Coach told the Professor how one of his star players was dating Gail and how proud he was of her also. He went on to tell her how long he knew her. All the way back to t-ball. Professor Fiao got a feeling that this was more than a chance meeting and asked Coach if he wanted to talk privately in her office. He chuckled and said her powers of observation were spot on. They walked to the elevator in the Madison Street building. As they went up to her office, the Professor thought to herself if she saw Coach before. She had a strong sense of déjà vu. When the elevator door opened, they walked to her office. Her office was filled with many native American artifacts. Coach noticed immediately as he asked her if he could touch the brownish stone she had on a shelf. She said of course and that it was just a stone. Coach sat in the chair and held the stone as he looked at it intensely. The Professor noticed and asked Coach what he saw in the stone.

Coach told the Professor, "Many stones are just that stones. Some stones have special properties that unlock when the sun hits them." He held up the stone to the sun from her window and said, "You are correct that this stone is just a stone."

The Professor was puzzled why a baseball coach would have such an interest in stones. Coach saw the puzzled look the Professor had. He sat in the chair and told her that as a baseball coach, he had grabbed some dirt and felt many stones. "Sometimes a stone catches your eye and for some reason it just appears special or different from all others and then it appears on a shelf in a professor's office." Coach stood up and thanked her for helping Gail. He told her that she could always speak to him at any moment since he was on the NYU faculty list. She said she was grateful to have Gail working with her and that she would keep him in the loop with any happy news she would discover about Gail. Coach thanked her and left.

76

The sophomore year started for the trio with all of them knowing everything. The past summer was the best summer of their lives yet again. Gail was immersed in the story she was told by Professor Fiao. Ray and Henry continued to work on their baseball skills and were dreaming of winning the college baseball championship again. All were puzzled with the story but they had become used to being puzzled with all that had taken place in their lives. Gail reminded them that September 6th must be the next day they would discover something and they should expect some event to happen to one or all. Ray and Henry reminded her that September 6th was not only her birthday. All laughed and parted. Classes started in late August. All loved the classes they were enrolled in. Gail took on a full course load in archaeology and Native American classes. Ray and Henry continued on the path toward becoming a lawyer. They were also beyond excited at the start of fall ball in mid-September. When September 6th arrived, Ray decided to buy a piece of jewelry for Gail. He went shopping with Mannity and they picked out a beautiful wrist bracelet with colored stones. Henry also decided to get a gift for Ray. It was the baseball card the two of them took when they were in little league. It was a picture of the two of them together in a Met uniform. It had the dates and other made up statistics on the back of the card. Henry always kept the card because it had Ray as a shortstop and Henry as a centerfielder. He felt that since both of them had become stars at these positions on a championship college team that maybe the Met uniform was possible.

On the morning of September 6th, Gail was busy working at the Madison Avenue site. She met the Professor very early and the two were busy excavating deep in the bowels of the building site. The Professor found various artifacts at the same depth level. She was hoping to find more and more today. Gail had an inner belief that they would find something special today.

They were digging a few hours and then Gail had to clean up and leave for class in a bit. She then hit a solid object with her shovel. She had learned to dig softly and feel the dirt as you dig. The Professor heard the sound and they both looked at each other with so much excitement. They both started to dig with their hands. They couldn't reach whatever they hit with the shovel fast enough. They both kept digging and their hands met on a metallic object. The Professor turned a shade of white and asked Gail to stop digging. She whispered to her that they needed to be very careful about what this might be and who knew about it. She covered the spot with dirt and left the shovel on top of it. They both cleaned up and agreed to tell no one. Professor Fiao closed the dig from her workers and told Gail to return tonight at 9:00 p.m. Gail agreed since both had to go to classes. Meanwhile Ray and Henry met for lunch and had their typical birthday discussions until Henry discussed the card. Ray had always dreamed of playing for the Mets. Henry added that maybe the card was a sign that this dream may happen for the two of them. Before they finished lunch, Ray showed Henry the bracelet he bought for Gail. Henry loved the colors and asked Ray how he picked out such a beautiful piece of jewelry. He told Henry how his mom helped him. Henry smiled and said he should have known that. Ray was going to meet Gail at the coffee shop a block away. Ray was a bit nervous. As he met Gail in the coffee shop, the two wished each other Happy Birthday. Gail was speaking about her morning class and Ray decided to tell her how special she was to him and gave her the bracelet. Gail loved it. Right after they kissed, Coach was walking into the coffee shop. Gail jumped up and showed Coach the gift. Coach said it was beautiful.

He also said, "Did anyone notice all the colors on the bracelet? It had some blue, red, green tones with a clear brownish color." Coach reminded them that maybe the colors are significant on this day. He wished both a Happy Birthday and asked them to tell Henry also if they see him. Gail sat and stared at the bracelet and wondered if the colors were just a coincidence. Ray grabbed her hand and told her nothing they do was ever a coincidence and they need to just live in the moment and stay on the path.

She kissed him and said, "Please do not ever talk like Coach again." She wanted to tell Ray what she thought she discovered this morning with the Professor but she decided to follow Ray's, I mean Coach's advice, and just follow the path for the moment. Henry went to his dorm and was studying. His bear started to walk across his desk. Henry found it strange because it appeared to him that the bear wanted to get his attention. The bear never did that before. It just pointed to where he should go. Henry gave the bear his attention and the bear noticed. The bear then walked to his baseball bag and entered it. He fell asleep in his glove. Henry picked up the glove and just couldn't figure out what the bear is trying to tell him. Henry texted Ray and Gail a picture of the bear in the glove. Ray and Gail ran back to the dorm. They got their bears and met Henry. When Ray got his baseball bag, the bear was already in his glove. Ray and Henry placed their gloves with their bears on the floor next to them. Gail took out her bear and it walked toward Henry's bat and stood motionless as it wrapped itself around the nob of the bat. The three of them could not figure out what the bears wanted them to know other than it had to do with baseball in some way. Gail finally decided to tell Ray and Henry what she possibly found today and the story she was told from Professor Fiao. She told them that she was going to meet the Professor tonight at 9:00 p.m. Gail hoped the numbers would be the clue and they would finally have some kind of answer tonight. Ray and Henry agreed and also were excited that maybe, just maybe their baseball dreams were part of the story.

Gail left the dorm room around 8:00 p.m. Ray and Henry told her to make sure she kept them in the loop and to be careful. After all, digging was not her specialty. Gail told them she would and asked them to try to play with the numbers tonight to figure out the next day or time. Just as she closed the door, she reminded them that maybe numbers were not their specialty. She took the subway and was thinking about everything. She put her hands in her pocket and felt her bear. She guessed the bear walked into her jacket and was a clue to her that tonight may be significant. She got off the train and walked to the building. She met the Professor in the elevator. Gail looked at her phone and noticed the time was 8:35 p.m. The Professor noticed her bracelet. She told Gail that she met Coach. Gail told her that Coach had always been a significant part of her life. She smiled as she looked at the bracelet and told her Professor that Ray gave her the bracelet. The Professor hugged her and told her she was very happy for her. Gail paused and said she is very happy with her life also.

They got to the business of digging. Gail let it out that today was her birthday and the Professor smiled and wished her the best birthday ever! The Professor had very specialized tools to help get the box out without damaging anything. She let Gail have the moment of taking it out from the earth. Gail looked at her watch and saw the time was 10:00 p.m. exactly. Gail knew 10:00 p.m. would be the time of discovery. The Professor had a moment of incite. She was perplexed at the reason Gail would be looking at her watch during a moment so big as this. She put the box down on the ground and asked Gail what is really going on. She told Gail how strange it was that a baseball coach comes to have a talk with her and notices the colors of the stones in her office. She said he spoke in riddles and it was hard to believe he was just a baseball coach. Gail stuttered and was having trouble explaining without revealing anything. Then the bear walked out and sat on the box. The Professor for some reason was not surprised or scared. She was happy to see this bear. She did not realize it walked out of Gail's pocket onto the box. She believed it was released from the rock. They took the box and the bear to her office, not the clean room. She did not want any record of the possible discovery today on camera until she knew what she discovered. When they reached her office, the bear walked from the sealed container to Gail's pocket. Professor Fiao looked at the bear in amazement. Gail said that she would have to trust her for the moment. She told the Professor that she would explain everything when she felt it was the right time. She suggested that the two of them clean the box and see if this is the box with the treaty sealed inside. For some reason, the Professor felt at ease trusting Gail. She agreed to move on with one condition. The condition was that she must be told whenever it would help move the discovery forward. Gail agreed. She told the Professor that the numbers nine, six, zero and one have always been around in her life. Birthdays, addresses, times, events could all be predicted in some way with these numbers. The Professor wanted to know why 10:00 p.m. would be a predicted time? Gail reminded her that her birthday was today, September 6th and 10:00 p.m. fits the numbers.

The Professor could not resist by adding, "What about the bear?"

Gail smiled and said, "That is a story for another time."

Gail and the Professor worked for hours cleaning the container. They discovered a lock. The lock had a dial with no apparent numbers on the small dial. It was late and they were tired. The Professor locked the box up in her desk and drove Gail back to the dorm. Gail went up and told Ray and Henry all that was discovered. Ray and Henry added that nothing happened to them on this special day. School was rolling and fall ball was adding to the legend that Ray and Henry were building. NYU never had such a schedule. They were playing UCLA, Florida and ending with Vanderbilt at Citi Field. As the month moved on, NYU won every game with Ray and Henry just doing magical things every game. Crowds started to come just to see the "Brooklyn Boys". The last game of the fall was on Oct 9th at 6:00 p.m. Citi Field was packed as if it was a regular baseball MLB baseball game. Gail was sitting on top of the dugout. Coach waved to her to come down into the dugout. She was a bit taken aback but Coach told her and security he wanted her to sit next to him in the dugout. As NYU was warming up, Coach asked Gail if she understood the date and time. Gail smiled and nodded. Coach said he expected something to happen today that would change the course of all their lives. Ray and Henry homered in the last inning to win the game. They were mobbed on the field as if it was a world series. Mannity was so happy but Manny was filled with all the joy a father could have at this moment. After the fanfare died down, Coach waved to his two stars to come over. He was with a gentlemen and Gail. Gail finally hugged Henry with happiness and then Ray. Henry was more surprised than Ray. Coach introduced the gentleman to his stars. He was a scout with the NY Mets. Mr. Narseeca. He said he had never seen so much talent in men so young. He told the two of them that he was offering them a chance to play for the NY Mets. He wanted them to sign a contract at the end of the year and start playing minor league ball in June at Coney Island. The three jumped around the field with the joy of a child.

Coach said, "They needed time for the moment to set in and to discuss this with their parents."

Mr. Narseeca agreed and gave the Brooklyn Boys his card and told them he expected to hear from them shortly.

Ray and Henry changed and skipped the team bus ride with Coach's approval. They met Gail outside the stadium. They had to be alone and discuss all that has happened. Manny called Ray many times. Ray had to answer. He knew his dad was beyond proud. He answered and after his dad had his moment of fatherly joy, he told his dad he had to go now. Gail made them walk to a park located near the stadium by the bay. Ray and Henry for once in their lives were speechless. Gail told them how proud of them she was. She even admitted that while she was not a great baseball fan, it was clear that "her guys" had a specialness to them on and off the field. Ray asked if any progress had been made on opening the box without destroying the contents? Gail told them they cleaned the box but the lock had no numbers and was all blank on dial. Henry wanted Gail to bring the two of them to her professor and explain all that now had happened to them and explain how the numbers kept appearing in their lives. Ray was a bit weary of the idea. The discussion turned to the unbelievable offer of the two of them leaving college to play professional baseball in Brooklyn after the semester and college season. Gail even sat back and could not believe the opportunity they had. Henry could not keep anything back any more. He had been living by the idea that the Coach had told them. He had lived his life and stood on the path. Henry wanted to have a discussion with the Coach, all of them and the Professor. They all agreed to this idea. They were however stuck on how to pull this off without the Coach or the Professor saying no. They decided to speak to Coach tonight and see if they could continue to be truthful to him. They all agreed to celebrate this event and called all their parents and met at a local bar. Hours into the celebration, Coach walked into the bar. Henry noticed and whispered to Gail that he must have them wired for sound at all times. Gail chuckled and playfully hit him but she added she had become accustomed to him showing up at the time they needed him. Coach was welcomed by all and he joined them. As the evening continued into the early hours of the next morning, Coach asked if he could speak to his trio alone for a moment. The families agreed and they moved toward the back of the bar far from anyone. Coach started with how he had been so proud of his young trio and the stars had chosen very well. Henry stopped the usual pleasantries and wanted to know if all that had happened had anything to do with them and their abilities or are they pawns in this cosmic play? Ray and Gail nodded in agreement with Henry. Coach paused and looked at his trio with love and respect. He said the time had come for his young birds to learn and make a decision about what path they would fly.

Coach asked his trio a simple question. "If many people have the same talent, why do some rise to greatness and others not? The talent that the three of you have is not what is important. What you have is a purity of heart and a sense of fairness combined with a natural stick-to-it-iveness that the numbers have chosen to right a serious wrong. The talents have always been yours. However, they are part of a path that must be taken by the three of you willingly."

Gail jumped in and told Coach about what was found in the dig with the Professor. Gail wanted to have all of us meet with the Professor and discuss all that had happened.

Coach agreed but countered with a simple question to all of them. "Do you believe that Professor Fiao was not also chosen to be a part of this path? The numbers have never let you down. Gail, you need to have a good night sleep and tomorrow work with Ray and Henry and let me know why Professor Fiao is a part of the story. If you trust the numbers and your ability, I will expect a call from you on a certain day." Coach said he had to go and get some sleep. "After all, someone as old as I am must have his sleep."

All went back to their beds and had the best sleep of all their lives. They went to sleep dreaming about all the dreams that seem to be coming true for all of them. When the afternoon came the next day, they all met in Gail's dorm after lunch. Gail got to work on the numbers. Ray and Henry were also paying close attention and trying to figure out how the Professor fit into the numbers. They started by reading her story on the NYU website. They played with numbers and saw no pattern for hours and hours. Henry then started singing out loud a song from Michael Jackson. Henry loved his music. He was singing the song ABC is as easy as 123. Gail asked him to stop but immediately jumped up after the words came out. She yelled that Henry was a genius. Ray started singing the song then and was waiting for Gail to acknowledge his genius. Gail got a piece of paper and a pencil. She wrote out the alphabet and matched the letters with numbers.

Henry yelled out loud, "How do we miss these things, Gail?"

Ray jumped in, "Tisk, tisk, tisk, Gail."

Henry then added that he was not surprised. It was October 10th at 6:09 p.m. Ray was keeping his discovery for a moment to show off to his best friends. He was working on the next dates to be concerned about. He wrote it down and placed the paper in his pocket hours ago. When Gail stopped praising Henry's singing ability, Ray decided this was his moment to show off his mental abilities. He took out the paper and showed his two friends the date he expected something to happen. They all agreed it made "number sense," but you never really know. Ray joked about how his moment didn't seem to matter. After a few minutes Gail and Henry hugged him and gave him the praise he so wanted in the moment. Gail then dialed Coach's number while she sat in a chair with a huge smile on her face. Coach answered and after they exchanged pleasantries, Gail decided to use pop culture on Coach instead of just explaining it all. For once, she wanted to have the upper hand in a conversation. She asked Coach if he knew the any songs from Michael Jackson. Coach responded by singing, "A,B,C." Gail was shocked. Coach added that he had been on the path for many, many years and had heard many singers come and go. However, Michael Jackson was his second favorite singer. Coach then told Gail that he spoke to the Professor in the past. Before he ended the phone call, he told Gail that the next events must happen in their proper time.

"You must be focused on living your life and being the best person you can be at all times." He then added, "You will have to deal with my two loveable knuckleheads also!" As the call ended, Gail sat down and for some crazy reason a conversation she had with Mannity many years ago popped into her head. Henry had to go study and Gail asked Ray to go to his house with her. The two hopped on the train and called Mannity. Mannity loved the opportunity to make dinner for her "kids." Gail asked Mannity if she remembered the story she told her when she was a kid in little league? Mannity said of course she did. Her Coach was so funny and supportive of her playing but the time was different. Girls just didn't play baseball then. She got up and dug out her old baseball pictures. She had a team picture. The date on the picture was June 9th. The year was rubbed out. Gail took the picture and stared at the Coach. The Coach had a beard and a mustache but she could swear somehow it was someone she knew. She kept this idea in her head and did not share it. Instead she handed it to Ray and asked if the Coach looked like any famous person he knows. Ray said no. Mannity looked and also said no. Gail let the moment pass. She did not want to sound stupid in front of anyone without more evidence, if this was even true.

As the days and weeks passed, Ray and Henry had much to decide. Would they leave school at the end of their sophomore year and chase their dreams? Would they stay enrolled in NYU and play college baseball? Manny told Ray to chase his dream of playing major league baseball. Ray felt this advice was not the best since his dad was blinded by having his kid playing in MLB. Besides, he did not really know all that had been going on. Henry and Ray knew they needed to talk to Coach. They called and asked if they could come to his office. Coach said of course and he expected them. Ray and Henry knocked on Coach's door.

They entered and made themselves comfortable. They all sat around the conference table. All were quiet. Coach broke the silence by reliving the fantastic fall baseball season they had and how it ended with an offer of a lifetime for his "two boys".

Ray and Henry jumped in by discussing the fall season also. Ray decided to just ask the question. He asked, "Coach, what do we do now?"

Coach sat silent for a moment. He then responded with a question. "Why do you think the stones gave you this ability?"

Henry said he believed his stone magnified his abilities but he had the ability to begin with. Coach turned to Ray and just looked at him. Ray agreed with Henry but he added that the stone gave him the strength to use his abilities to help achieve a goal.

Coach then asked, "What is the goal?"

Henry answered that the goal had always been to try to play professional baseball. Coach sat back in his chair and waited. Ray responded that he wanted to sign with the Mets but a part of him felt he would not be on the correct path. Coach then started to talk in a language Ray and Henry never heard. The two bears walked out of their backpacks and walked into Coach's hand. Henry watched but asked Ray if he remembered taking the bears. Ray shook his head no. Coach smiled at the two bears and said something very softly that only the bears could hear. The bears nodded and walked over to Ray and Henry. They stared at them. They then walked over to a baseball on the shelf behind Coach. They pointed to it. Ray and Henry were relieved. They wanted that answer! They agreed to call Mr. Narseeca soon and tell him they will sign the contract. The bears then jumped up in what could only be described as a joyful jump. They walked back into the backpacks. Ray decided to ask Coach about the language he spoke to the bears. Henry added that he had never heard any language like that and they have been in a language melting pot, NYC, all their lives. Coach said they had not lived as long as him in NYC and it was a language that was hundreds and hundreds of years old.

While Ray and Henry were coming to terms with choosing the path they would take in the future, Gail continued to work hard at her studies and at the dig site. She became a star in the archeology department at NYU. She was reading many books and mastering the concepts that were being taught. She was using her memorizing abilities by mastering everything she read. A great skill to have when you are studying many different Native American tribes. At the dig at Madison Street, she pressed on digging and searching for more evidence. She also worked on opening the metal container they found. This was a painstaking process. Professor Fiao allowed Gail to work alone also. This was a big step for the Professor and Gail. They moved from a teacher-student relationship to a more friendly relationship. Gail admired the Professor. The Professor was so happy to have someone like Gail join her in this adventure. As the fall term came to an end in December, Professor Fiao asked Gail if she had some extra time to work on the container today. Gail jumped at the invitation. She felt the Professor had an idea or thought she was going to share since she never received such a personal invitation from the Professor before. The two met in her office and the Professor took out the container from the airtight safe. The Professor noted how hard Gail had worked on cleaning the box. She was impressed by the skill Gail had shown in this process. The dial was much more clearly visible. However, the numbers or whatever should be around the dial was not. The Professor asked Gail if she had any ideas about how to proceed. Gail felt that the

Professor did not have any idea on how to proceed at the moment. Gail put on her white gloves and grabbed the container. She stared at it for a few moments. She placed it gently back on the desk. She said she had an idea. She ran into the lab next door and got a small measuring tape. She measured the circumference of the dial. The Professor just sat back and watched her protégé go. She then drew the same circle with the exact same circumference on a piece of paper. Gail then reasoned that the numbers on the dial had to the same distance apart as they were today. She measured the distance between numbers on her combination lock on her book bag. She then multiplied that distance and matched it to the circumference on the dial. She sketched the numbers on the paper dial she made. It came out to twelve numbers. The Professor was quite impressed at the simple and common-sense approach Gail took to this problem. Now, the Professor wondered aloud about how to mark the dial accurately without any damage to it. Gail put on her white gloves and started to measure the dial quite accurately. She said she could use a dissolvable white ink and place a tiny line using a tiny thin brush for a tiny mark for each of the twelve numbers. Gail thought this would take weeks. The Professor agreed and reminded her how the fall semester was over and she had a great project to work on for the next few weeks. Gail did notice that none of the others had been coming to work at the site. The Professor said she had all the workers she needed. Gail smiled and was so proud to have this project to herself. She hoped for answers on so many fronts.

Ray and Gail grew together since childhood. Their relationship was built on friendship and trust earned from growing together and sharing so many life experiences. Gail had always loved Ray. She waited for Ray to become mature enough to admit he had strong feelings for her. College changed Ray into a very mature and respectable young man. Not that he wasn't this person before. He just became more comfortable in his skin and was able to accept and act on his feelings for Gail. They were two peas in the so-called pod. They trusted each other and recognized the skills and abilities each had. Gail always knew Ray would become a baseball player. Ray always knew that Gail would become some type of academic star. The strange and unique part of this was Henry. Henry fit in like he was supposed to at all times. He was loved and respected by Gail and Ray at all times. Henry was the clown and the most honest of the three since childhood. Henry also needed Ray and Gail. They were his anchors. He turned to either one all the time for help or guidance. Henry dated and was quite popular on the college campus. He just didn't find his special someone yet. Ray always told Gail he wasn't looking. Gail always believed he was looking and sometimes was disappointed he didn't find his special someone. Ray always ended with that is why men are from Mars and women are from Venus. Gail asked her two favorite men to come see what she had been working on. Ray and Henry were busy trying to figure out what they could expect from their first professional baseball contract. They asked Coach to be their agent. Coach agreed to and told them not to worry. "Mr. Narseeca and I go way back and fairness will be the rule here."

Ray and Henry were still worried but they needed to work on something else to keep their mind off this. Gail told them they would not be disappointed when they came to the dig.

80

Ray and Henry jumped on the train and were surprised to see Coach on the same train. They walked over to Coach and asked where he was going. Coach asked his two stars to take a seat next to him. As the train kept moving along, Coach turned to his two stars and started talking about how taking the subway always reminded him about the long journey he had been on and the journey his "trio" was taking. As the doors opened at Canal Street, Coach showed some joy as he smelled his favorite food, dim sum. He told Ray he wished he could go and have some lunch and how dim sum is his favorite food of all time. Henry never had dim sum and thought this was a made-up name. Coach then turned back to the discussion and said their stop was approaching and just like a journey, he hoped this could be the end of the beginning. Ray and Henry knew better than to question the words of Coach. However, the end of the beginning sounded out of place to them since their beginning hadn't even started yet. The doors opened and the three exited the train to start the walk to Gail at the dig. Somehow Ray and Henry forgot all about the original wonder about Coach appearing on the same train at the same time as them. As they entered the building, Coach paused and looked down the street.

Henry asked, "Coach, what are you looking at?"

Coach kept looking down the street toward the river. Coach then appeared to prepare himself for a moment to enter the building. Coach finally answered Henry. He was looking down the street and remembering the way it was and it reminded him of a happier time. Henry agreed that Manhattan had changed a lot during the past decades. Ray broke up the moment by reminding them they had to take the elevator to meet Gail. The elevator doors opened and they met Gail in the clean room. Ray and Henry actually enjoyed getting ready to enter the clean room. Coach took a more practical approach to it and viewed it as a rather painstaking annoying process that one must do. Finally, they were all ready to enter the room. Gail opened the lock and all entered. Gail explained what she had been working on the past five weeks. Professor Fiao then entered the room. Coach nodded hello and the Professor winked back. All were ready for Gail. Gail explained all she had done. She showed them the container. It was as clean as it could be with the markings she made on the lock. Ray whispered into Henry's ear that today was January 6th and to look at his phone. Henry noticed the time was close to 9:00 p.m. As Gail told all that she believed the combination to be 1609, Coach turned to Professor Fiao and agreed with Gail's logic. Ray chimed in and had to remind Gail how he was correct about the date he predicted. The Professor told them that she had trusted Gail from the moment Gail asked her to just trust her. While this discussion was going on, the bears literally walked into the conversation. They walked onto the desk and turned to Coach. Coach bent down and spoke to them in a language no one understood. The Professor however saw some of the words she heard on some of the artifacts in her collections. She said to Coach this sounded like a Native American dialect to her. Coach said it was a language from the deep past that his family insisted never be forgotten. The Professor had many questions to ask in the moment but the bears took over. The bears walked over to the container after Coach finished speaking to them. Each assumed a position at the dial. When the last bear touched the container, the container appeared as new as the day it was made with the three bears posing in a protective pose around the dial. Gail rubbed the bear she believed was hers and thanked her bear for all the guidance and strength the bear gave her. The bear winked back to Gail. Gail had a sense of joy for the bear and entered the combination one, six, zero and nine. She heard a click and opened the container. The container contained a folded paper. Gail gently opened the folded paper and it was completely blank. The paper appeared quite old by its texture and appearance. The Professor wanted to take a tiny piece off of the top right corner to carbon date it. Coach asked to take the smallest piece possible. He said that another step was obviously required to obtain what they needed to see. As Gail gently folded the paper back into it original position, Henry jumped in and wanted to know what the bears would do if they put it back and closed the container.

Coach said to close the container and relock it. The trust the bears have given you has never wavered. Trust the bears in the same manner.

Gail closed the dial and the she heard the lock click into a locked position. The bears then jumped off the cover of the container and walked back to their respective backpacks. The trio had to go back to the dorm. They wanted to discuss all that has happened. The blank paper was very perplexing to all of them. Professor Fiao asked Coach if he could stay. Coach accepted her invitation to stay and wished his young people a productive afternoon. The Professor offered Coach a cup of coffee. He graciously accepted. She then let loose her emotions about the bears, numbers and all that she had witnessed. She told Coach that the worst of everything was that she could not tell anyone about this because no one would believe her. Coach chuckled and said he could explain much to her but she must accept that she was part of a greater good. A key part also. The Professor sat dumbfounded as Coach sipped from his cup of coffee. The Coach started with the London lecture. He showed her a picture of Mr. Narseeca. She recognized him immediately as the Professor giving the lecture in London. Coach told the Professor that this cannot be shared with the "kids." Coach added that he knew she was a very trustworthy person. She agreed not to share any information he would give to her. Mr. Narseeca had been a lifelong friend of his for many, many years. He decided to let NYU Brass become aware of the possible deed for the land that was given to the Canarsee tribe many years ago. Mr. Narseeca explained to Coach that a tribe in upstate NY won a significant legal battle gaining its lost land from an agreement it made with George Washington. Coach agreed that the time has come for the Canarsee to obtain the land stolen from them many years ago. He arranged to have the meeting with you.

"I made sure that my trio was on the path to meet you at the correct time and the correct moment for them."

The Professor was beyond amazed that her life had been part of a master plan. After all, she was a scientist. Coach then asked her to check her name with the numbers. Her name made it clear to all of them that she was to be trusted and be a part of the events that would unfold. The Professor had to bring in the bears. She added that they are very cute and loyal to the kids and yourself.

Coach said, "They contain the spirit of the Canarsee. They are loyal to all that they feel are working for justice and fairness. They speak the language of the Canarsee. I also speak that language with Mr. Narseeca."

The Professor wanted more information about the trio. Coach took his last sip from the coffee cup and then sat back and stared at her with a rather uncomfortable stare. He then explained to her that his trio had to face a large storm in the future. The road chosen for them would be very difficult. "They have been given certain abilities to help them face the coming storm. Our roles are to support them and help them prepare for the storm."

The Professor understood and was also no fool. She could figure out the rest of the story on her own. She thanked him for all he had chosen to share. Before Coach left, she told Coach that she now had a newfound love for bears. Coach responded that the bears held a special place in his heart as they reminded him of all that he had lost and what he may gain back in the future. Coach left as he thanked her for all she had done so far.

Meanwhile, the trio arrived at Gail's dorm. Henry was a bit angry at a blank piece of paper. All the events had led to this moment and when they opened a box from the past it had a piece of blank paper. Ray agreed with Henry but was much calmer. He felt that the paper was blank because they were not ready to read what it had to say. Some other process or event must be required to occur before they could read it. Gail thought there was more to the story here. She said she needed time to process this. The paper was blank because something else may be required for it to be seen. This something may be an event or something else. At this moment, Mr. Narseeca called Henry. He asked for a date and time they could meet with Coach to sign their contracts. Henry said he would speak to Coach. Mr. Narseeca reminded Henry that time was short. The college baseball season would be starting soon and the rules of the NCAA will not allow signings after February 1st. Henry said he would call him back shortly. Ray called Coach. Coach said January 9th at 6:00 p.m. in his office would work. He just spoke with Mr. Narseeca. The young men agreed and were beyond excited. When Gail ran over to hug Ray, she looked at her bracelet as she hugged Ray. She was so happy for them.

The Professor received a call from NYU Brass. They noticed that her expenses had dropped significantly. After all, only herself and Gail had been working for the last few months. They wanted to come down to the dig and see all that had been revealed since they last discussed the project. The Professor politely set up a date at the end of February. After she hung up the phone, she sat in her chair and wondered aloud about what she would show them and tell them. She laughed to herself about the bears, Mr. Narseeca and Gail. She was most concerned about the lapses in the cameras. How would she explain the shutting off of the cameras? She had a few weeks to prepare. Prepare she did. After she told Gail, they went to work first on cleaning up the dig. Making it look the way it should. Both Gail and the Professor found that the love they had for their work helped them to arrive at all the answers they were going to give. When the day of the meeting arrived, Gail made sure to be working in the dig. When the brass arrived, the Professor called for Gail to introduce her as her "wonder student." The Professor asked Gail to explain all that has been discovered. They started with the drawings on the cups. Dr. Afi and Dr. Oaf were quite impressed. It was a clear sign that the moment may have occurred. The Professor then took out the container. Dr. Afi put on his white gloves and noticed how old the container was. He was clearly having a moment of professional joy. Dr. Oaf asked if it had been opened. The Professor said they had been working on the dial. They did not want to destroy the container. All agreed that this must be a last resort after all options had been tried. They offered to have it taken for a CAT-scan. The Professor countered that she had already worked on a date for this at NYU facilities. It would be done but she then explained the work Gail had done with the dial. They agreed that more time must be given to open the container and hopefully find the most important piece of the tale, the treaty. They also agreed with the idea of only having the two of them working given all the progress that has been demonstrated.

They ended with a simple question, "If you found the container, then why are you still digging?"

Gail was speechless. Professor Fiao broke the silence by explaining that in all her experience searching for artifacts from the past, when you find a key object there are always unexpected objects to be found also. The Brass agreed and stated they would return in a year or two. They added that if the container was opened, they must be informed immediately. After they left, Gail and the Professor were happy that they never asked about the cameras. The Professor added that they may have just decided it was not the time to ask. Either way, they had more time to work on the riddle of the paper.

As Gail was working for weeks with the Professor, the young men had a meeting with Mr. Narseeca and Coach on January 9th in the baseball office at the stadium in Coney Island. Ray and Henry arrived a bit early. They were beyond excited. They were shown to the office and the two of them just stared out the window at the baseball field. The parachute tower and the beach was just beyond centerfield and rightfield. Left field faced the rides at Coney Island and Nathan's hot dogs. They could not believe they were going to play here as professional baseball players. Coach and Mr. Narseeca came into the room. After they all sat down and discussed the upcoming NYU baseball season, Mr. Narseeca asked the young men if they understood the changes that would occur if they sign. Ray and Henry said they did. Coach added that they would no longer be enrolled in NYU after this semester. They would no longer be allowed to play in the NCAA. They again stated they understood and that this was what they always dreamed of. They wanted to play for the NY Mets. At this point, Coach opened the door and had their parents come into the room. Manny could not hold back his pride. He was beaming. Henry's mom was also filled with joy. Mr. Narseeca stated they would be offered a very generous contract matching all they accomplished last year. They were offered a standard minor league contract for one year with a two hundred and fifty thousand dollars signing bonus. The contract and money will be executed one day after the NYU baseball season ends. Coach added, hopefully in early June after the NCAA championship. Ray and Henry signed. Coach and Mr. Narseeca stepped out for the families to take pictures and enjoy the moment. Mr. Narseeca asked Coach if they had any idea of the future they may have. Coach stated that they have shown a rare trait of consistency during all the time he had known them. He believed they would continue to be who they were and baseball would not change them. Ray and Henry celebrated with their parents at Nathans of all places. Mr. Narseeca added that it was a standard NY Met tradition to come to Nathans to celebrate a signing. Ray and Henry wanted to tell Gail together. They hopped on the subway and raced back to the dorm. Gail was so happy for them. As she hugged Ray again, she stared at the stones in her bracelet. Gail had never been so happy as she had been in this moment. She then hugged Henry and told him she never had any doubts that he would make it. Ray laughed but wondered if she doubted him. Gail enjoyed the little seed of wonder she planted in Ray's head.

As March came, the baseball wonder twins were picking up exactly where they left off. NYU was winning game after game and Ray and Henry actually started to become the talk of the city. Never had NYC embraced college sports since the 1980s when St. John's basketball was king. NYU baseball games were consistently being sold out and the Mets offered NYU to play at their minor league stadium. The stadium held eight thousand people and again all games were sold out. Ray and Henry marched their team to exciting wins against all the best college teams. Somehow, both young men also managed to maintain solid grades in their classes. Their teammates were in awe of the discipline they exhibited. Even Coach at times was impressed. Ray and Henry remained the young men he always knew. They did not allow all the fame and notoriety to change them. Somehow, they stayed grounded. A whirlwind of events had taken place during the last few months. The trio had a weekend of no activity planned. Henry asked if he could just go and sleep for the weekend. Ray and Gail said goodbye as he left. Ray and Gail sat together and just shared bits of all that had happened to them. Gail was looking at her bracelet from time to time and Ray noticed. Ray loved the attention Gail showed her bracelet.

As the end of the semester approached, Ray and Henry were proud of the grades they were going to receive. They did not take cupcake classes and took the classes they needed to follow their respective paths. As always, Gail was at the top of her class and mastering everything she took. Gail worked hard the last few months at the dig. She was looking for something to help her understand why the paper was blank. At this time they received the carbon dating info from the paper and it was shown to be the proper age for the paper to be the treaty. Gail and the Professor found many artifacts at the same layer they found the container. The artifacts were pieces of cups, a small canoe, a piece of a paddle, some Dutch plates and a metal plate engraved with a picture of the Canarsee. As each discovery was made, the Professor made sure to share this with the NYU Brass. Gail always added that they had nothing to worry about. Dr. Afi and Dr. Oaf fit the numbers. The Professor used her fingers as she figured it out. She smiled and told Gail that she was relieved but as a scientist she continued to have trouble trusting the numbers.

Gail added that June 9th was coming and she was sure they would move the project forward. Meanwhile, Ray and Henry were progressing in the College World Series again. Their celebrity status was rising above last year. The news about them signing with the Mets also added to their status. Games were packed events. Unheard of in NYC for most college sports. The dates were posted for the College World Series, June 1st to June 6th. In a unique moment, the NCAA chose Citi Field as the one-year home for the College World Series. NYU made the series and every game was a sellout. Ray and Henry were the baseball darlings of the town. They remained unchanged by their meteoric rise to celebrity status. They just kept working. They always heard Coach in their head about keeping to the path. After NYU won the series on June 6th, they reported to the Mets the next day and were playing in Coney Island. They never missed a beat all summer in the minor leagues. They were even bigger stars. It was clear to all that they will be called up by the Mets in September. All during the summer, Gail kept reminding her men that this may be a test about their character. Gail wanted her men to be up to the challenge and hoped they would not allow the sudden fame and fortune to change who they were and affect the task at hand.

As the fall came, Gail was set to graduate a year early. It was very strange for her. This was the first time in her life that Ray and Henry were not at her side in school. Ray always called her when he was on the road and at home they always made time for each other each day. Henry remained the bachelor but put a lot of energy into honing his baseball abilities. While Ray and Henry outwardly stated they did not miss school, to themselves and Gail, they were a bit scared and missed school. After all, how many twenty-year-olds leave school to play for the NY Mets? All summer the trio had many meetings to figure out the meaning of the blank paper. They worked on hundreds of ideas and each one seemed to be a dead end. As the summer ended, Henry reminded his compadres that each time they reached an impasse like this, something stepped in and helped them. The moment Henry finished his words, someone knocked on the door. Ray opened the door and it was Coach. It was a very eerie moment for the trio. Coach sat down and congratulated all of his trio. He was beyond impressed with all they had accomplished. He told Gail how she should be so proud of all the work she put in to graduate a year early. Coach then turned to Ray and Henry and told them that Mr. Narseeca told him they will be called up to the Mets on September 6th. As crazy as it sounded, Gail was the most happy. For the first time Ray and Henry appeared worried. Coach reminded them to believe in their talents. He also told them that he was hired as a batting coach for the NY Mets. Ray and Henry were so happy and so relieved to have Coach on this journey. They were young men doing something very few young men have done successfully. They needed and wanted Coach in their corner. As Coach said his goodbyes, he told Gail how beautiful that bracelet was. He said the colors reminded him of a proud past that he sorely missed. Coach then left. Gail took her bracelet off and looked at the colors. She asked Henry if the colors matched the colors of the stones that started all of this. Henry said it did but her bracelet had much more of the brown tones that matched the brown stone he still had. Gail looked at the bracelet and had an idea. She asked Henry to bring the stone over. Henry said he always had it in his bag. He opened his bag and handed it to her. The color matched her bracelet. All of a sudden, the three bears walked over to the stone and pointed to it. Gail moved the bracelet and the stone to opposite places. The bears moved and pointed directly at the stone. Gail jumped for joy. She knew what she had to do. She grabbed the three bears and the stone. She called the Professor and told her to meet her at the dig. All agreed. What troubled all was that today was September 1st. Then the Professor called back Gail and said she would meet them at 6:00 p.m. Henry then said he finally felt good about the numbers for once. They all took the train together to meet Professor Fiao at 6:00 p.m. The trio was unaware that Professor Fiao called Coach and Mr. Narseeca also. All were coming to the dig. They all hoped this would be the night they solved the puzzle.

All arrived on time and while there was some shock, they were somewhat relieved that everyone was there. Ray and Henry were a bit perplexed about Mr. Narseeca being present but they trusted Coach and had a feeling he played a bigger role in all of this than they understood at the moment. When they entered the Professor's conference room, Gail explained that her bracelet had been the key all the time. Ray was proud and wanted to make a joke but he was at a loss for words in the moment. Gail said the brownish tones in her bracelet matched the color of the stone left from the original stones they discovered at the Rock. Gail asked the Professor to go back to her office and bring the container.

When the Professor returned, she placed the container on the desk in front of Gail. Gail started to take out the stone and the three bears. Coach and Mr. Narseeca stood up and asked Gail to pause for a moment. Mr. Narseeca looked at Coach. Coach appeared to have nodded in agreement. Mr. Narseeca then explained that they had waited for this moment a very long time. Everyone needed to understand that this journey was about to enter the most difficult phase.

He looked at each person and said, "If you are not willing to see this journey to its appropriate end, please do not proceed."

Henry stood up and said he wanted to do the right thing. He felt he owed Coach so much for attaining his dreams. Ray agreed. Gail not only agreed but added that she had felt compelled to see this journey to its rightful end. Even the Professor felt this was always about something bigger than a treaty. They all sat down and Coach asked Gail to do whatever she felt she needed to. Gail took out the three bears and allowed them to walk to the container. They went into the dial of the container. Gail then entered the combination: one, six, zero, nine. The container opened. Gail put on her white gloves and carefully opened the paper. She then took out the brown stone and ran it over the blank paper. The paper suddenly filled with words. It was written in Dutch. Coach asked for white gloves. Professor Fiao gave him a pair. He got up and stood next to Gail. He looked at the signature of the Dutch representative and the fingerprint of the Canarsee. He spoke to Mr. Narseeca in the language of the Canarsee. They appeared to be overjoyed. The Professor ran a language program on her computer to reveal what the paper states. It clearly was the treaty the Dutch signed with the Canarsee. The Professor now had to ask. She told them that she met Mr. Narseeca in London and now he was a lawyer and a scout with the NY Mets! She asked for Coach and Mr. Narseeca to explain.

Coach agreed that they deserved an explanation. "Mr. Narseeca has always been the most trusted person I have ever known. He has been by my side for hundreds of years. We were both present when this was signed. I am the medicine man Danckaerts. I was present during all of this. As I saw the slow death of my people and my culture, Chief Mamalis asked me to use a spell that was never used. I had only learned part of the spell. When I gathered what was needed for this spell, I waited for the appropriate time. That was the night of Chief Mamalis death. I went to the rock after his death and started the spell. Something went terribly wrong. I saw streaks of light enter the four stones. Another streak was a bit different. It was a strange yellow. Little did I know that my friend, Mr. Narseeca had followed me. He was very concerned about me. The strange light passed into myself and Mr. Narseeca. We passed out for what appeared to us as forever. During that time it was revealed to us that we must prepare to save our people by learning all about the new world that has come. For a time we were depressed as we watched our people die. We decided that we had to save our people somehow. We studied all we could. We learned as much as we could about our people. The few who managed to survive left our sacred lands in Brooklyn. They merged with other local tribes. As we learned we waited for signs. We looked for events but none came. As the years passed, we learned we were not aging. We didn't question it. We had no answer other than those strange rays of light that hit the two of us. We decided to continue to learn the American ways. We have amassed a significant amount of wealth during the last four hundred plus years. Then I met my special trio in t-ball. Your birthdays were a coincidence at first and then I learned that Mannity was working at the museum. As I learned more about the three of you, Mr. Narseeca learned about the treaty being searched for by NYU. We both knew where it was but we needed to understand if this was the time for the Canarsee to come back. The numbers, events and our other contacts all believe this could be the moment."

They all sat dumbfounded. Ray spoke first by saying, "This is so difficult to believe yet it all makes sense to me now."

Gail asked how the bears came to be. Mr. Narseeca asked Coach if he could explain. Coach smiled and said of course. Mr. Narseeca said the strange light that passed out of their bodies didn't stop at that point. It hit the container with the treaty that Coach had at the moment. "When we passed out, the container was gone. The three little bears were sleeping next to us." Coach frantically was looking for the container and the bears pointed in the direction. "We followed the bears to the container in lower Manhattan. Each time we tried to pick it up and leave without being discovered by the Europeans, the bears shook their heads quite violently. We learned not to question our bear friends and have accepted that they are as much a part of this journey as we are."

Henry took all of this in and wondered out loud about the next step. "What do we do now? We have the treaty? Do you really believe the American legal system will hand over pieces of NYC to you?"

Coach said that was never part of the journey. "We do not mean to harm and will not harm any people. We want to obtain our sacred land and build a society to restore our people. Our people belong here. Our sacred land is in Brooklyn."

Mr. Narseeca jumped in and added, "We have kept track of our people. There are only one hundred and seventy people who have the blood of the Canarsee in them."

He looked at all and said everyone in this room had the bloodline of his forefathers from Brooklyn. Coach asked them to put the treaty back in the container. He asked the Professor to provide him with a translated copy. She agreed. Coach then added he needed a little time to organize the next steps. As the container closed, the bears jumped out and they hugged Coach and Mr. Narseeca. They walked back to Gail and went into her bag. Coach asked if he could hold the stone for a few days. Henry said he didn't have to ask. Coach said he had to. The stones chose very wisely by picking his trio. Mr. Narseeca agreed and then turned to Gail and added how different he looks clean shaven.

91

Coach and Mr. Narseeca called Ray and Henry the next day. They reminded them that they must continue to focus on their baseball path. Ray agreed but said it would be difficult. Coach added that their baseball path was an integral part of this journey. They must remain focused on playing for the NY Mets. It had been lost on Ray and Henry that the Mets were in a chase for the playoffs and were only a few games out with a few weeks left to the season. Coach added that he and Mr. Narseeca would be away for a few days. They boarded a plane for the Netherlands. As they sat on the plane together, Mr. Narseeca turned to Coach and said with a bit of worry, "Do you believe what we need is in the archive?"

Coach responded after a long pause. "I have to believe it. Otherwise, why are we still here?"

Meanwhile Ray and Henry became national sensations. They were building a miracle in Flushing. As September came to a close, the Mets made the playoffs due to the play of the "Brooklyn Boys". They were young and played baseball with an enthusiasm and skill that had not been seen in years. Ray actually stole fifteen bases in four weeks! Henry was batting over four hundred! The first round of the playoffs were set to begin on October 6th in Los Angeles. Gail was enjoying her sudden celebrity status at the games. Her picture was shown many times on TV. Even Professor Fiao who is not a baseball fan, loved going to the game with Gail. For the moment, Gail, Ray, Henry and the

Professor took some time to just enjoy life. Meanwhile Coach and Mr. Narseeca in late September needed a few days to visit Amsterdam. They made an appointment at the treaty Depository of the Netherlands. The Government of the Netherlands was actually quite helpful and after everything was explained, they found a copy of the treaty. They acknowledged that the treaty was valid for one day only. They made a copy of the treaty and applied their official seal to it. Coach and Mr. Narseeca thanked them for their help and boarded the next plane back to NYC. After all, they wanted to see the Mets final push into the playoffs also. The Mets won the first and second round of the playoffs. They were now in the league championship series. Ray and Henry were becoming baseball heroes quickly. T-shirts about the "Brooklyn Boys" were selling all over the country. Coach was back in the dugout and even he was enjoying this special ride. The championship series was a nail biter each game and somehow, the "Brooklyn Boys" did not disappoint. The Mets made it to the World Series. NYC was abuzz with excitement. Ray and Henry were asked many questions about everything. One question about their nationality was asked. They responded that they were part everything including Canarsee. The pride they stated that in was noticed by all who saw it. Suddenly they were more than just young kids playing baseball. They were Native American baseball players. The narrative was not lost on the media. It was brought up many times as the series rolled on. The magic that Ray and Henry displayed on the field became infectious to all the Met players. They swept the series and all were on their way to the parade in the canyon of heroes.

A few days after the series win, the emotions died down a bit. Gail wanted to get back to the journey. She asked everyone to meet in the Professor's office. Coach and Mr. Narseeca wanted to get back to it to. It became clear to them that this might be the time to start the case. Ray and Henry had brought the Canarsee tribe alive in the minds of America. Coach took out the copy of the treaty the government of the Netherlands gave him. The Professor took out the container and they watched the bears do their thing. Professor Fiao was like a little child watching the bears go into the dial of the container. It just never got old for any of them watching the bears. Gail held the stone over the paper as they all wore white gloves. The Professor was prepared this time. She had computer programs installed to read both papers at the same time to see if they were an exact match. When she did her thing, it was demonstrated that they were an exact match! Now Coach wanted the fingerprints matched. Professor Fiao anticipated this moment and also had a program installed to check this. The fingerprints match also. Mr. Narseeca could not hold it any more. He started to speak in the language of the Canarsee, stopped himself as he looked at all, he said he had nothing to hide from his family. He stated that they needed to match Coach's fingerprint to the fingerprint on the treaties. Gail was the only one not surprised. She always had a feeling it was Coach. When the fingerprint was checked, it matched. Mr. Narseeca suddenly changed the manner in which he would speak. Right before all their eyes, he became a trial lawyer. He expressed all the reasons why this was the time to file for their sacred lands in the first district court in lower Manhattan. He stated that they had a valid treaty in place. One from each party. No one denied that the land was stolen from the Native Americans. They also had two national celebrities who had brought the consciousness of the Canarsee to America. Coach agreed. Coach wanted everyone to know that when this is filed, no one must ever speak to the media or anyone about the case without the approval of Mr. Narseeca. Coach made it clear that they must allow the courts to do what they needed to do and trust Mr. Narseeca. When the treaty was placed back in the container, the bears walked over to Mr. Narseeca and gave him much love. They then walked back to Gail's bag. Mr. Narseeca informed them that he would work on filing the case in the next few weeks. He advised Gail to go back to school and work on her classes. He asked Professor Fiao to inform her brass that the project was now working on matching the paper to the past. Ray and Henry were asked to speak to the media anytime they were asked to and keep the spirit of the Canarsee alive in the media to the best of their abilities. Everyone agreed and all went to work.

For many months they worked on their daily lives and the assignments each were given. When spring came, Mr. Narseeca was ready and prepared to file a motion with the Bureau of Native American Affairs and the District court in lower Manhattan. Ray and Henry were all the buzz in spring training in Florida. They had become the lovable faces of baseball. They were young, talented, bright and media darlings. Both made sure that every opportunity that popped up to bring up their Native American heritage to the forefront was taken advantage of. Google searches about the Canarsee were getting huge numbers. Ray and Henry were also enjoying the new phrase applied to them. They were now the "Canarsee Brothers from Brooklyn". Gail and the Professor continued to research the treaty and the NYU Brass was informed about the court filings. NYU was very nervous about this filing. After all, NYU currently owned almost all of lower Manhattan. They also seemed to finally trust Professor Fiao. She kept reassuring them that this was not about taking anything from NYU. The brass decided to allow her to keep working and they gave her the ability to grant classes to allow Gail to obtain her bachelor's degree in archeology and Native American studies immediately. They gave the honor of informing Gail to Professor Fiao. They also awarded Gail a doctoral acceptance with a full scholarship to continue to work with Professor Fiao as her mentor. When the Professor informed Gail, her joy was childlike. Gail and the Professor had grown to be much more than Professor and student. They were true friends with a mutual respect for each other. Gail found her place in the world at this time of her life. She wanted to work with Professor Fiao. The Professor finally found someone who matched her passion for her work with a creative genius that she admired. The group decided to take a few days to meet in Florida. Ray and Henry were in Port St. Lucie for a few days with spring training. Mr. Narseeca made the arrangements. Later that night they all met at the Met training facility.

Coach and Mr. Narseeca explained to the group that the filing had shaken the Federal government. In the filing, they stated that they could prove beyond a reasonable doubt that the sacred land of the Canarsee was taken in a series of illegal actions. In return, they were asking for a site of 960.1 acres of their sacred land in the current section of Canarsie Brooklyn that was almost entirely made up of NYC buildings. "We stated that we will pay for the costs of relocation. We will also pay five times the market value for the few private homes that are there."

This time the Professor broke the silence and said, "All of this seems fair. So why does Coach have such a sour look on his face?" Mr. Narseeca asked Gail to truly look at Coach. He asked her to use her trained eye. Gail looked and looked. She then gasped for air when she noticed. Coach had a strand of gray hair that he never had before. Mr. Narseeca congratulated Gail. Coach said that he believed he had finally aged a little bit. He then continued to explain his worry. He believed that his journey may come to end with this court case. Mr. Narseeca added he had also aged just a bit. He took out a very old, small, leather briefcase form his modern briefcase. He gave the four of them all the required passwords. He stated that they have accumulated over one hundred billion dollars' worth of wealth over the last four hundred-plus years. This leather case contained all of the papers, stocks and passwords to access it. "I have added your three names to all accounts in the event Coach and I have an untimely passing. I must add that the Federal government after my filing did do their diligence and discovered our immense wealth. I am worried that they may ask some questions about the dates of purchase and age of certain accounts. This is why we have asked all of you to meet here. The case will start soon. All of this may come out. We are giving each of you the access codes to the safe deposit box to this case. We keep it at the Oneida Native American reservation bank. The person to speak to is on the paper that I am giving to each of you. The bank is located in upstate NY."

This was a lot to process. Some time passed with worries and fears being expressed. Coach allowed all to just vent. It appeared they all needed to do this at this time. Then Coach responded, "All of us will be facing a firestorm of hate, worry and fear. We must always stay above this and be sure to always do the right thing. We must trust that the spirits of the Canarsee that have set this in motion for over four hundred years will deliver us."

With that, the cell phone in Mr. Narseeca's pocket rang. It was the clerk of the Federal Court in Manhattan. He set a trial date of May 1st and jury selection would begin on April 15th.

When Mr. Narseeca placed his phone down, he looked at all and stated how happy he was to be associated with such fine upstanding people. Coach added that he could not be happier to face this journey with the people in this room.

As jury selection began for this case, Mr. Narseeca decided to ask the judge and the Federal government for a judge trial with one condition. The courtroom must be open to the public at all times. The Federal government immediately agreed. The judge turned to Mr. Narseeca and asked him if he was sure this was how he would like his case to proceed.

He agreed and then added, "Whatever is decided here, I must also add that the Federal government will not file appeals and will abide by the decision."

All agreed and the trial was set to begin on May 1st. As Coach and Mr. Narseeca prepared the case of the Canarsee vs the Federal Government of the United States, Gail and the Professor worked on understanding the treaty. They analyzed it and read it over and over. It clearly stated that the government of the Netherlands would leave lower Manhattan and acknowledge the land of the Canarsee in return to helping to resettle in another location. It also stated that all dealings will be with Chief Mamalis or any representative of the Canarsee tribe of their choosing. This was the key. The treaty also acknowledged that the people of the Netherlands had done wrong by taking land that was not theirs to take. It was signed and sealed by the Governor of the colony. Gail and the Professor knew that Coach and Mr. Narseeca understood this. The Federal government has no knowledge of this treaty and may claim ignorance. How can a country abide by a treaty it never knew about? Gail and the Professor took the time to start researching the Oneida tribe. If they were trustworthy enough to be the custodian of the Canarsee wealth, they may also have clues on how to deal with this claim. The Oneida fought in the courts for years against the Federal government to obtain its land in upstate NY. As Gail researched the process, she discovered that the money to fund this process was given to the Oneida by Coach and Mr. Narseeca. In 1794, a treaty was signed by no one less than President George Washington. It stated: "The United States acknowledges the lands reserved to the Oneida, to be their property, and the United States will never claim the same nor disturb them." Professor Fiao texted this info to Coach and Mr. Narseeca. They both thanked them for the history lesson they forgot. They were ready for May 1st.

Ray and Henry asked the Mets for a day off to be in court on May 1st for this trial. The Mets granted the day. This had the effect of putting the trial right in front of the American people. Mr. Narseeca opened the trial by discussing the events that led to his people almost being killed off and their sacred lands taken. He moved on to the treaty the Canarsee had with Netherlands. This was a bolt of worry for all in the courtroom. He ended by citing the United States has a history of honoring treaties with Native American tribes much later than when they were signed. He expected this to be the case in this treaty. This was all over the sport news outlets. After day one in the court, the next date was set for May 8th. This happened to be an off day for the Mets. When they all entered the courtroom. Ray and Henry were surprised to see that all their teammates were in the courtroom. Coach sat with Mr. Narseeca smiled and stated in the native tongue of the Canarsee how they just may see this journey to its rightful conclusion. Mr. Narseeca took out the copy of the treaty that he obtained from the government of the Netherlands. The Federal government immediately claimed they had no knowledge of this treaty. The judge agreed and stated this to Mr. Narseeca. Before he spoke he looked at Gail and called her to the stand. She took the oath and explained to the court the current research she was doing on the Oneida tribe. She had a copy of the treaty President Washington signed and gave to the Oneida in 1794. Then Mr. Narseeca added that somehow the Federal government "forgot' it had this treaty until 1998 when the Oneida produced the copy it had. The Federal government then took ten more years in courts before it honored the treaty signed by no one less than George Washington. The judge understood the point. He turned to the Federal lawyers and asked that if the treaty was found to be sound and legal, would the federal government then accept the outcome of this treaty? The government asked for time to examine the treaty they knew nothing about. The court was dismissed until June 1st.

Meanwhile, they all noticed how many more gray strands of hair Coach and Mr. Narseeca suddenly had. Coach even had a small wrinkle on his forehead. They all agreed that the new grays actually made them look much more wise and regal. It was a good look in the courtroom. Mr. Narseeca informed all that they would have to be prepared with the bears, the container and the stone for June 1st. All were worried. Coach as always added that they must trust all the tools they had been given and all would work out. June 1st came and Mr. Narseeca had a small box decorated with the artwork of the Canarsee on his desk. Ray and Henry were not present. It was agreed at this time that they were not needed. The court room was packed and filled with cameras. The Federal lawyers started their case by stating the examined the treaty and spoke to the government of the Netherlands.

"The treaty is a valid treaty with respect to the Netherlands. However, we discovered a strange paradox that we would like answered in this court." The judge nodded and asked the Federal representatives to proceed. "We ran the fingerprint on the treaty in their extensive database. The fingerprint is in their system. It puzzled us very much. How can a fingerprint from 1609 be in the database of fingerprints of the U.S. government? As a matter of fact, the person is in this courtroom. He is sitting next to Mr. Narseeca."

The court let out a ball of emotions. The judge demanded order. As order was restored, Mr. Narseeca asked if he could call Coach to the stand. As he went to the stand and placed his hand on the bible, Coach stated his name. "My name is Danckaerts."

The judge asked for his full name. Danckaerts turned and stated this was his full name. He was then seated. The lawyer for the Federal government got right to it. He asked how could this be his fingerprint? Danckaerts stared at him for a moment. He then looked straight at him, and stated he was there at the moment the treaty was signed. People in the court immediately started to laugh and mock him. The lawyer then stated that he would be over four hundred years old! At this moment the box on the desk of Mr. Narseeca started to shake violently for all to hear.

Danckaerts smiled and stated that the contents of the box would explain much. "However, are you willing to face a reality that you never considered?" The courtroom went silent. The judge demanded that the cameras be turned off. Danckaerts reminded the judge that this was not part of the deal he made. The cameras remained on to the dismay of all except Danckaerts and Mr. Narseeca. Mr. Narseeca opened the box and the three bears made their grand entrance walking over to Danckaerts.

They stood on the railing between him and the judge. For the first time they appeared angry. Danckaerts asked if he could explain his story. The lawyer was tongue-tied at the moment and agreed. Danckaerts explained how he was present with a trusted friend. "The treaty was given due to the people of the Netherlands feeling they were hurting my people. They saw the suffering from the new diseases that destroyed my people. They agreed to be resettled far away from anyone and return our lands to us for help with this resettlement. A copy of the treaty was given to me in a container. When I went back to my people, most were dead or going to die from smallpox. I discovered our chief, Chief Mamalis had passed also at the big rock. Next to him was a necklace of four colored stones. The spirit of the Canarsee was placed in these four stones. A strange ray of light then hit myself and my trusted friend. We were never the same after that. The bears found us and have been an invaluable companion to us during this trying journey to regain our sacred lands and restore the Canarsee to its rightful place at the table of humanity." As this was broadcasted, the world witnessed this in real time.

A rush of people arrived outside the courts in lower Manhattan. The judge stated that this was just not a believable story. The bears then walked over to him and pointed at the wall emblem behind him. They pointed to the phrase "In God we trust." Danckaerts smiled and stated that maybe the judge should have some faith in the words that are behind him and seem to always govern him. The judge wanted to stop the trial and digest all that had occurred. Mr. Narseeca jumped up and stated that his client must be allowed to finished his story. The rules and inherent unfairness that existed in courts seemed to melt away as the judge stared at the many cameras in the courtroom.

Danckaerts then stated, "The treaty was buried in what you

call lower Manhattan and was discovered by two archeologists at the NYU dig."

Mr. Narseeca walked over and handed the container to him. The bears walked over and went into the face of the container. The code was entered and stated for all to hear. One, six, zero and then nine. The container opened. The paper was slowly opened after Danckaerts put on the white gloves he had in his pockets. He asked for the brownish stone. He stated that this was one of the stones with the spirit of the Canarsee locked in it. He moved the stone over the paper and the treaty appeared for all to see. It was an exact match. Mr. Narseeca then asked for the judge to rule in favor of the restoration of the Canarsee land to the people of the Canarsee. The 960.1 acres along the shore of Brooklyn at the east end of Jamaica Bay. All financial issues would be repaid fairly as they had stated. The judge asked for a recess and stated he would make his decision on June 9th at 1:00 p.m. The court was adjourned.

109

Somehow, the court officers got Mr. Narseeca and Coach out with their box without anyone knowing. Apparently, the building was built with a series of underground connections to the subway many blocks away. They met at Gail's dorm. The firestorm hit. Every channel was covering the story. Even the President of the United States stated that he would be at the next court date. Ray and Henry were getting too many offers to be interviewed. Gail and Professor Fiao were worried that they may be in over their heads. Coach stated that they were all chosen for this point because of the abilities each of you have. "Do not lose faith in your abilities. Be who you are and always do the right thing."

Coach asked Ray and Henry to do an interview at Citi Field with the media. He asked them to answer everything honestly. "The truth is the truth. It is up to people to determine the level of their faith."

Mr. Narseeca asked Gail and Professor Fiao to be in the courtroom with them. He felt that they may be asked to discuss the discovery. He reminded them also to tell the truth at all times. He asked both to refrain from speaking to the NYU Brass until after the settlement was given. The settlement would have all the answers the Brass wanted anyway. All agreed. Mr. Narseeca looked at Coach and stated it was time to return to their home for the next few days. They had a home in the Canarsie section of Brooklyn that no one knew about. They asked Professor Fiao and Gail to come with them until the trial date. Gail stated she believed she knew the house. It was the small blue home with a small dock at the end of East 106 street. Coach chuckled.

He asked, "How did you reason this out?"

Gail stated, "You seem to have let all the events of the day affect you. The house number is nine."

Mr. Narseeca let out a big laugh and agreed it had been a day they had been waiting for over four hundred years. All slept soundly and prepared for the next day.

Ray and Henry were having a great spring baseball season up to this point. Ray was leading the league in average and hits. Henry was the league leader in home runs. They were going to give the press conference at 1:00 p.m. since they had a game that night. They were not nervous about this. When the conference started, Ray and Henry asked if they could tell the story and then allow for questions. All agreed. They started by discussing how Coach was their t-ball Coach. He taught them everything about baseball. He has always been there for them from t-ball to high school to college and even in the majors. Henry then discussed how they joined the gardening club with their best friend, Gail. They found the colored stones at the big rock in front of Madison HS.

"Three of the stones seemed to dissolve into each of us. The remaining stone, the brownish one, was the stone you saw in court. We have been checked many times by doctors and we have no apparent issues. However, the stones gave a sense of purpose and drive to help our people. We are only here because of our baseball ability. It is a shame that we could never get any audience about the tragedy our people faced when the Europeans arrived and how we were almost wiped out from it. Our sacred land is almost completely an abandoned property with a few

NYC administrative buildings and a few private homes on it. We are just asking for a small piece of our land to be returned so that we can build a thriving community and help the people of NYC."

The questions then centered on the stones. Ray explained that this was many years ago in high school and he had had so many medical check-ups and blood draws that nothing had physically changed him or hurt him. Henry believed the spirit helped them use the gifts we had by giving them a sense of purpose in a long journey. Ray asked for the media to not dismiss all that had taken place. Many things could not be explained at the moment. That did not mean things were not true or hurtful. "Our people have a right to exist with all of you and live in our sacred land."

Henry was worried since the room went quiet. One reported stood up and stated he hopes the Canarsee can put the horrible events of the past behind them and go forward in peace. The conference applauded. As the days passed and June 9th approached, it became apparent that all the coverage and the unexplainable yet quite loveable bears became the topic that all were talking about. Suddenly the plight of the Canarsee mattered. They went from a footnote in the history to a symbol of something magical where the past injustices can be mended. The moment was not lost on the President of the United States. He held a press conference and stated how he will be attending the trial on June 9th. Coach and Mr. Narseeca were finally basking in the moment in their home in Canarsie. They waited over four hundred years and were just relaxing and waiting for the final moment to occur. Gail was quite impressed at their inner peace before the ruling that was going to come soon. Ray and Henry requested the day off and it was granted. Gail came over with dinner on June 8th. Coach and Mr. Narseeca reminisced about her apparent lack of t-ball skills when she was a child. Gail blamed the inability on her coaches. Gail then had to ask something that was always on her mind. She asked Coach if Ray, Henry and herself did all that Coach believed they should have done. Coach smiled from ear to ear and responded that the stars could not have chosen any three better for the current task and the future tasks that were coming. Gail was honest enough this time not to hold back her thoughts. She added that it was ending the way it began, with more questions than answers.

It was a typical bright sunny day in NYC on June 9th. All of lower Manhattan was packed awaiting the verdict. As 1:00 p.m. approached, the President of the United States entered the courtroom and sat next to the Federal lawyers. He did walk over and shake the hands of Coach, Mr. Narseeca and Gail. He stated how proud he was of all of them for taking up this cause. When the judge started the proceedings, all sat down except the President. He remained standing and requested to speak to the court. The judge looked at Mr. Narseeca and he nodded in complete respect. The President turned to the gallery which was filled with people and cameras. He started with how the Canarsee had not been treated fairly in history. He added that many of the events were not caused by the United States since it did not exist at the time, however, to ignore a moment when a wrong in the past can be fixed would also be wrong.

"I have spoken with the senate leaders and the mayor of NYC. We have agreed to honor the spirit of the treaty. We will cede the 960.1 acres of land to the people of the Canarsee. We will hold you to your statements that fair and equitable financial issues that remain will be worked out in an equitable fashion for all. We are honored to have the Canarsee take their proper place at the seat of the American table." The President turned to the judge and stated that he had no need to rule. The United States considered this matter closed.

The emotion that was released in the courtroom and outside was filled with joy. Many felt that finally something from the past was righted. Coach, Gail and Mr. Narseeca just held each other and cried. No one noticed in the moment that the bears left the box and walked over to the President and the three bears stood up on their hind legs and clapped. When they finally did, the moment seemed magical. It is rare when people accept things they cannot explain without question. Very rare.

That night Coach and Mr. Narseeca insisted all come to their home in their restored sacred land. The future of the land and the tremendous amount of work to be done was not to be discussed at this time. Coach talked about how the journey was so long and how his trusted friend, Mr. Narseeca was always at his side working toward this day. Coach then took out a small box. He opened it. He took out three necklaces. Each had stones that were red, blue and green. He told them that he found this box at the site you have been digging at hundreds of years ago. "We had always wondered why it had three necklaces. We now understand the meaning. The three of you restored the sacred land of our people. You always used your gifts in an honorable way. We have always believed that the spirits of our people would lead us to the right path. Never did we know that you three would be the embodiment of all that we needed and hoped for. Mr. Narseeca and I would like the three of you to wear these necklaces as a reminder of all the good you have done and also the hope that you three will always be around to help our people."

As Coach and Mr. Narseeca placed each necklace around their necks, it appeared to all of them that the stones took a greater shine for a few moments…

Printed in the USA
CPSIA information can be obtained
at www.ICGtesting.com
LVHW051549220524
780810LV00001B/38